Fatal Fall
(A Miranda and Parker Mystery) Book 18

Linsey Lanier

Proofread by

Donna Rich

Copyright © 2021 Linsey Lanier
Felicity Books
All rights reserved.

ISBN-13: 978-1-941191-70-5

Copyright © 2021 Linsey Lanier

All rights reserved. Without limiting the rights under copyright reserved above, no part of this publication may be reproduced, stored in or introduced into a retrieval system, or transmitted, in any form, or by any means (electronic, mechanical, photocopying, recording, or otherwise) without the prior written permission of both the copyright owner and the above publisher of this book. This is a work of fiction. Names, characters, places, brands, media, and incidents are either the product of the author's imagination or are used fictitiously. The author acknowledges the trademarked status and trademark owners of various products referenced in this work of fiction, which have been used without permission. The publication/use of these trademarks is not authorized, associated with, or sponsored by the trademark owners.

FATAL FALL

It's been almost two weeks, and Holloway still isn't back from his ex-wife's book tour. To top it off, Miranda is being hounded by her crusty Aunt Lu in Minnesota about her mother's death.

The last thing Miranda wants is to delve into her past again. Worst of all, Parker has gone on a case without her. Now she's royally PO'ed.

So PO'ed, she travels to Chicago on her own to prove her mother's death was an accident and get her aunt off her back.

But was it an accident?

And is the killer now coming after Miranda?

THE MIRANDA'S RIGHTS MYSTERY SERIES
Someone Else's Daughter
Delicious Torment
Forever Mine
Fire Dancer
Thin Ice

THE MIRANDA AND PARKER MYSTERY SERIES
All Eyes on Me
Heart Wounds
Clowns and Cowboys
The Watcher
Zero Dark Chocolate
Trial by Fire
Smoke Screen
The Boy
Snakebit
Mind Bender
Roses from My Killer
The Stolen Girl
Vanishing Act
Predator
Retribution
Most Likely to Die
Sonata for a Killer
Fatal Fall
(more to come)

MAGGIE DELANEY POLICE THRILLER SERIES
Chicago Cop
Good Cop Bad Cop

OTHER BOOKS BY LINSEY LANIER
Steal My Heart

For more information visit www.linseylanier.com

CHAPTER ONE

Nerves roused in the pit of her stomach as she drove through the rusted iron gate.

Through the darkness, she rumbled over the dirt road to the shadowy building in the distance, ignoring the bumps and the gnarled limbs of unkempt oaks lining the path. At last she reached the building.

It was huge.

In the twilight she could see it was made of stately red brick, like some old elaborate Victorian mansion. Tall columns that must have once been white were now faded and overgrown with ivy. They barely supported a dilapidated upper porch.

What was this place? she thought as she climbed out of her car and approached the wide front stairs.

The sign etched in stone over the entrance answered the question. "Midwest Hospital." That was the name she'd been given. This was where she was convinced he was. All her research had pointed her here.

But this place was abandoned.

Squinting up at the sign above the entrance again, she noticed the name wasn't centered. There were more letters, hidden by the ivy.

She took out her phone, switched on its flashlight, and held it up. Stretching as far as she could, at last she made out the rest of the letters.

And as she read them, her heart stood still.

"Midwest Hospital...for the Insane."

Now it all made sense.

Stepping back, she peered up at the steeply pitched rooftops. Spike-topped turret towers stood on either side of the structure. She dared to move around the overgrown hedges and peek around one of the towers.

Towards the rear of the building she saw a chimney.

Smoke curled from its cap. And there was light in one of the back windows on the third floor.

Her breath caught.

He was here. Somewhere inside this place. Hiding.

Once again she examined the entrance. She shouldn't go in there alone. She should get the police first.

But she'd been to the police. No one believed her. No one would help her.

Her boyfriend had left two months ago, tired of her obsession over her mother. Her father had died four years ago from grieving so long over the loss of his wife. Her sister was in London directing plays.

She was on her own.

But she had her conceal-and-carry with her in an ankle holster. And she had to find out what happened to her mother.

Determination fueling her, she marched back around and up the steps to the massive front doors.

She gripped the handle, and to her amazement, it opened.

She stepped inside and found herself facing a huge double staircase in the style of some elegant hotel from the last century. A dim light from somewhere gave the brass facing of the landing an eerie glow.

The air was uncomfortably warm, making the large space feel close. The place was decayed and filthy, and the odor of dust and mildew made her suddenly feel ill.

Should she turn back?

She couldn't. She'd come too far, waited too long.

Ignoring the sickening sensation, she studied the staircase on the right. It should lead to the room she saw outside.

Again, up she went.

She ducked under the thick cobwebs that hung from the ceiling like veils. Beside her, the walls were a mishmash of torn wallpaper and shedding plaster. Below she could tell water damage had rotted the floor, but somehow the dusty stairs held her weight.

Finally she reached the landing. How to get to that room she'd seen outside?

Blinking in the shadows, she spotted an open archway. She stepped through it and found herself in a long corridor. There were rooms on either side, more like a hospital than the entrance. A very old hospital. Again the paint on the walls was cracked and peeling. More cobwebs hung from the corners. There was no decor.

The light from caged bulbs overhead made the hall even more sinister. But the evidence of electricity told her someone was living here.

Eyeing the darkened doors on either side as she passed them, she decided she didn't want to know what was behind them. The light she saw from the window had to be farther down.

About midway through the corridor, she noticed an odd scent in the air. Cinnamon?

Her blood ran cold.

But how? And why? It didn't make sense. Not here.

And then she saw a light under the next door. Not allowing herself to think about what she might find, she opened the door and stepped inside.

It was a kitchen.

An old fashioned one with a mid-century fridge and stove. Warm, almost cozy. And in the oven a pan of something was baking. She bent over and saw the white frosting on top. Cinnamon rolls.

Again, she shuddered.

She turned her head and saw a door to another room opposite the stove.

It had an opaque pane, but she could see light through it.

Before she lost her nerve, she hurried across the room and opened it.

Here the smell was antiseptic, sterile. Large round lamps on poles flooded the place with light, leaving her blinking. The air was suddenly cold, making her shiver.

Her vision cleared, and she realized there was a hospital bed in the middle of the room. Someone was lying on it, covered by a sheet. There were tubes running into the person connected to three different IVs hanging from poles. One looked like it had blood in it. There was a monitor as well. Its screen was dark.

As she approached the bed, the smell in the room, mixed with the scent of cinnamon from the kitchen, turned nasty and had her nearly gagging.

But then she saw the face had been uncovered. It was a woman. Young. Pretty.

Extending a finger, she dared to touch her cheek. Cold. Icy. Gray. She gasped out loud.

The body under the sheet was dead.

Suddenly an arm slipped around her throat. It was a man's arm, clad in the sleeve of a white lab coat.

"What do you think you're doing here?" demanded a raspy voice behind her.

It was him. She knew he was here.

Instinctively, her hands grabbed at the arm, trying to pull it away.

She found her voice. "I'm here to find out what you did to my mother."

"Your mother?"

"She died twelve years ago, just like that woman in that bed. What did you do to her?"

Softly he chuckled in her ear. "I'll show you what I did to her."

The arm around her throat grew tight. She couldn't get to the gun in her ankle holster. She struggled hard, but she couldn't breathe. Lights began to twinkle behind her eyes.

And the last sensation she felt was the man pulling her backwards and out of the room.

CHAPTER TWO

"The new bodyguards Daddy brought on last month seem to be acclimating well."

"Uh huh."

"And we've acquired several new clients."

"Mmm."

"Larry Cutler's at the top of the IIT class so far."

"Nice."

Miranda Steele sat at her desk in her office on the fifteenth floor of the Imperial Building, with Gen across from her in a guest chair. They were supposed to be going over reports, but Miranda couldn't pay attention.

Instead, she was scrolling through the unanswered texts on her phone.

Hey, Fanuzzi. What's going on?

Miranda had sent that one last Monday. Two days after the baby shower and the big blow up. She'd thought Fanuzzi would have calmed down over the weekend, but her friend hadn't replied.

Next text.

Hi there. How are you doing?

Miranda had sent that one last Wednesday. No answer.

Hey, wuzup?

She'd sent that text two days ago.

Not even a nibble.

With a sigh, Miranda stared out the window. Her heart was still stinging at Fanuzzi's words to her. "I don't think I can be friends with you anymore, Miranda Steele." She could still hear the bitterness in her voice. "Do you think we're children? That we're stupid or something?"

She never should have told Fanuzzi she and Parker had paid off her house, but she'd thought it would make her happy. Keep her from overworking herself.

Instead, she'd lost her best friend.

Parker said Fanuzzi would get over it, and things would be better after the baby was born, but Miranda wasn't so sure.

Gen emitted a matching sigh.

Miranda turned to her and saw she was staring out the window, too.

She was dressed in her usual dark business suit, and every strand of her short platinum hair was in place, but Parker's office manager daughter looked pale, and she definitely wasn't her take-charge self.

Miranda didn't have to ask why. She'd witnessed the explanation herself in a Saint Simons bookstore not long ago. Curt Holloway, her old work buddy, had broken Gen's heart by falling back in love with his ex-wife.

When they'd decided to retire last month, Miranda and Parker had left Holloway in charge of the Agency. But Holloway had called and told them he needed a week off to serve as a bodyguard for Audrey Wilson, his ex-wife. She'd written a book and wanted him to go on tour with her.

My Ordeal. Sheez.

Like a fool, he dropped everything here and ran after her like a wounded puppy. It was pitiful.

Parker had given Holloway one week.

That week had run out six days ago. Tomorrow would be two weeks since Holloway had abandoned his job.

Oh, he'd called—around eleven pm on the last day of the week he'd been granted. He'd said the tour had been extended and he needed more time. He said Audrey needed him. He couldn't leave her.

Yeah, Miranda knew what that conniving shrew needed him for. Not the least of which was the sick thrill she got from twisting him around her little finger.

Parker had given Holloway the time, but Miranda knew he was going to replace him. He'd been spending a lot of time with Judd lately, preparing him for the takeover. It wouldn't be long before Parker installed Judd as the new CEO, and they could get back to their retirement.

Unless Parker was having the same second thoughts about retiring that she was.

And then there was Wesson. Miranda hadn't heard a word from her colleague since she'd okayed her month-long sabbatical. That was up now. Wesson should be waltzing through the Agency door any day now.

But she hadn't made an appearance yet.

Actually, she'd asked for extended time off. She'd said "maybe" a month. She must have meant longer.

Gen got to her feet and straightened her skirt. "Well, I guess we're done here. I have a meeting in a few minutes."

Maybe she should say something to the poor girl. Offer some comfort.

Miranda cleared her throat. "Gen?"

"Yes?"

The stiff wariness that crossed Gen's face told Miranda the woman wouldn't welcome any advice from her. Not about whether to take notes with a gel pen or a ball point, let alone Curt Holloway.

Before Miranda could get out, "never mind," her cell rang.

"You'd better get that." And as if she were glad to escape, Gen scooted out the door.

With a huff, Miranda looked down at her screen.

She didn't recognize the number. It wasn't a local area code. No doubt somebody was calling to tell her they had a six million dollar check waiting for her, if she'd just give them her bank account information.

Instead of hanging up, she decided to give the caller a piece of her mind.

She swiped the green button. "Listen, you. If you don't stop scamming people, I'll find out where you are and give you six million smacks in your ugly face."

"Well," said a vaguely familiar voice. "Is that any way to answer your phone?"

Miranda blinked, feeling suddenly very uncomfortable. "Who is this?"

"You don't know?"

Miranda thought a moment. Crusty voice. Midwestern accent. No, Minnesotan accent. She sounded a lot like her mother.

A chill went down Miranda's spine. "Aunt Lu?"

"Of course, it's your Aunt Lu," the woman barked.

Miranda scowled. Why in the world would her Aunt Lu be calling her? She hadn't seen her in aeons. Not since…her mother's funeral.

"Uh, good to hear from you."

"Is it?"

"Sure." Miranda didn't know what else to say. "How are things in Rochester? You're still there, aren't you?" Rochester, Minnesota was where her mother and Aunt Lu had grown up.

"Of course, I'm still here. Where else would I be? And I suppose you're down in Atlanta with that gorgeous hunk of a husband of yours?" She said it as if she thought Miranda was having a party, and she hadn't been invited.

How did Aunt Lu know where Miranda was? And that she had a gorgeous hunk of a husband?

Her tone made Miranda's shoulders go stiff. "As a matter of fact, I'm at work. Did you call for a specific reason?"

Aunt Lu huffed out an annoyed breath. "How can you even ask that?"

Miranda stared at the phone, wondering if Aunt Lu was getting a little senile.

"I keep reading in the paper about this case that you and your husband have solved, and that case you two have solved. Every time I do, I want to scream." She was getting loud.

"Calm down, Aunt Lu. Where exactly did you say you were living now?" Maybe in an assisted facility?

"Ha. The idea never crossed your mind, did it?"

"What idea?"

"About what happened to your mother?"

"My mother?"

"Seventeen years ago, your mother died."

When Miranda was twenty and still married to Leon. "Yes, Aunt Lu. I know when my mother died."

"Well, if you don't care about what happened to her, I do."

"What are you talking about?" Miranda's mind raced. When her mother passed away, a neighbor had called her and told her she died of a heart attack. That had turned out not to be exactly true.

"Your mother died under suspicious circumstances."

The neighbor, Mrs. Gavinski, had explained it to her when she and Parker had gone to Chicago trying to find her daughter. "It wasn't suspicious circumstances. It was an accident."

"Hah."

Hah? That was what Mrs. G had told her. "Look, Aunt Lu, I—"

"I want to hire you."

"What?"

"I want to hire you and your husband to find out what happened to Hilda."

Find out what happened to Hilda? Well, didn't that just beat all. She didn't want to work for Aunt Lu. She didn't want to dig up the past about her mother's death. She was supposed to be retired.

She had to get off the phone. "Sorry, Aunt Lu. I think we're going to be busy for a while."

There was a lot of paperwork to do.

"You don't care what happened to your own mother? What kind of a daughter are you?"

Miranda clenched her teeth.

The kind who had married a creep when she was sixteen to get away from her. "I'll have to check with Parker. Let me get back to you."

Before her aunt could hurl out another accusation, Miranda hung up.

Staring at the phone, she tapped her foot. Aunt Lu wasn't giving up. She'd be calling back. She'd get Parker to talk to the woman. He could sweet talk her into hiring someone else.

Slipping the phone into her pocket, Miranda headed out her door and made the ninety-degree turn to Parker's office, which was right next to hers.

She rapped on the framework, but there was no answer.

She stepped inside and turned to the desk, expecting to see Parker's gorgeous sexy frame in his usual dark suit and tie, with his perfectly styled salt-and-pepper hair.

He wasn't there.

His laptop was gone, too. That was odd.

That morning Parker had said he was expecting an early call, so they had taken separate vehicles to work. But he should be done with that call by now.

Then she remembered the meeting Gen had mentioned. That's where he had to be. She'd just mosey over there and talk to him for a minute.

She made her way to the conference room and poked her head in.

In their crisp dark business suits, Gen, Detective Tan, and Judd were seated in the ergonomic chairs around the long glossy table, notepads and laptops at the ready.

Gen scowled at her. "What is it, Miranda?"

"Is Parker in here?"

She raised an indignant brow. "Does it look like he's in here?"

His usual seat was empty. "Isn't he supposed to be in this meeting?"

"No."

Why not? she wanted to ask, but then thought better of it. "Okay, thanks."

Feeling befuddled, she turned around and moved down the hall to the water cooler where she came to a stop.

Now what?

Miranda had to think of something before Aunt Lu called back. She didn't want to talk to her again. She didn't want to think about her mother or what had happened to her. It was over and done with, as far as she was concerned.

Her father had abandoned them when she was five, and Miranda's mother had always been cold and distant, and sometimes downright mean to her. She left her alone most nights because she was working, and if Miranda did something she didn't like, she'd go after her with a belt and lock her in a closet.

Miranda's thoughts drifted back to the day almost two years ago when she and Parker had gone to the house where she'd lived with Leon. They'd talked their way inside and gone up to the attic. They'd found her mother's trousseau in an old trunk, along with a manilla envelope.

The envelope had contained a document that listed Hilda Steele's cause of death.

Miranda's head shot up as she snapped her fingers. That's what she needed.

The death certificate.

But where was it now? Parker had taken the envelope when they'd left the house in Chicago. She remembered that clearly.

It must be in the penthouse somewhere.

Glad she had driven her speedy Corvette to work, she headed out to the parking lot.

CHAPTER THREE

An hour later, Miranda had gone through every cupboard, drawer, and hiding place in the penthouse. Not that there were many.

Parker kept things sparse here. Probably most of their important documents were on his computer. He might have scanned that death certificate, but surely he wouldn't have discarded the original.

Standing in the wide expanse of the living room, Miranda eyed the floor-to-ceiling bookshelf and scratched her head.

He wouldn't have stuck it in a book, would he?

Then she remembered the state he must have been in when he'd left the Parker mansion. They had just broken up. He'd probably taken only what he needed and left anything of hers behind. Why not just call him and ask?

She winced.

Even though their relationship was stronger than ever now, their breakup was a painful episode she didn't want to rehash with him. Still, it was probably likely her mother's death certificate was somewhere in that big house.

Okay, it had ten bedrooms, but she could find it. She was a detective, after all, wasn't she?

Locking up, she took the elevator down to the parking deck, got in her car, and drove to Mockingbird Hills.

A few minutes later, she pulled into the driveway of the Parker estate. Today she ignored the willow trees, the huge mansard roof, the majestic balustrades that never failed to intimidate her, and hurried up the landscaped walk.

Coco answered the big elaborate door of the big elaborate mansion with a wooden spoon in her hand. An apron was wrapped around her waist—which was so big, Miranda wondered if she was having twins. Or maybe triplets.

"Hi, Miranda. What's going on?" Coco said in her feminine Southern voice.

Miranda couldn't stop staring at her stomach. "When are you due again?" She hadn't kept track.

Coco laughed. "Not for another few weeks. Why?"

"Never mind. I have a favor to ask. Mind if I come in?"

"Of course, not. I always think of this big house as yours, anyway. Yours and Wade's, that is."

Miranda didn't know what to make of that statement. So she just stepped into the expansive foyer with its tall austere paintings, antique furniture, and broad mahogany staircase.

"Is Estavez home?"

"He's in court today."

"Everything still—you know—okay between you two?" Less than two weeks ago Coco thought her handsome Latin lawyer husband had been cheating on her.

Today she beamed with happiness. "Couldn't be better. Though I've had to put my paralegal studies on hold for a bit."

"Oh?" Miranda sniffed the air. Cinnamon. "Are you cooking? Didn't mean to interrupt."

"I'm making apple fritters for Joan. The Oglethorpe's oldest daughter is having an engagement party this evening."

"Oh?" Miranda repeated. The Oglethorpes were neighbors here.

"In fact, I'm doing almost all the cooking for Joan now."

That didn't sound good. "How come?"

Creases appeared in Coco's pretty brow. "She's not doing well with her pregnancy. The doctor's warned her she might have to have total bed rest, but she just won't hear of it. Antonio and I offered her the bedroom off the kitchen. I told her she could supervise from there, but she said no."

"Yeah, she doesn't take kindly to charity."

So Fanuzzi wasn't taking it easy, even after Miranda's confession. She wished the stubborn woman would talk to her. Then she could fuss at her about not taking care of herself, and Fanuzzi could stop speaking to her for that.

Coco brushed back a strand of her pretty blond hair. "I need to get back to the kitchen. Want to come watch?"

Coco knew better than to invite her to help cook. "Actually, I came here to look for something."

"Oh, what?"

Miranda didn't want to go into detail about her mother. "A document I think Parker might have left here. Have you seen anything like that?"

"Um...there were a few boxes we found here and there. I think Antonio—" Coco's nostrils twitched. "Oh no. The oil's burning. I thought I turned it down." She spun around and ran down the hall. As she disappeared around the corner, she called out. "Just look wherever you want. You know your way around."

Yeah, she did.

Miranda stared at the empty hallway, then turned around and made her way to the big mahogany staircase. Her stomach tightened. That staircase looked even more humongous and intimidating than when she'd lived here. She hadn't climbed it since the day she'd left the Parker mansion more than eight months ago.

But her mother's death certificate had to be in one of those upper rooms. She was sure of it.

And she wasn't going to find it just standing here.

Taking a deep breath, she put a foot on the first step and forced herself up.

CHAPTER FOUR

Starting on the third floor, Miranda tackled the Taj Mahal room first. Memories flooded her as she stepped into the high-ceilinged chamber and took in the teakwood, the tiger skin patterns on the wall, the evocative paintings on the domed ceiling.

There was no scent of candles or lotus blossoms now.

The gold-tasseled pillows had been piled neatly on the red-and-black spread of the round bed. Apparently, Estavez and Coco hadn't used the room the way she and Parker did. Still, just the sight of it brought back all the delicious sensations Parker had given her here.

She loved him so much.

But indulging in erotic memories wasn't helping her right now.

Turning around, she opened the small closet and poked around in there. But there was nothing but extra blankets, pillows, and a bottle of body oil.

She went through the rest of the rooms on the third floor, then headed for the one Parker had used as an office on the second.

Here were the black lacquered credenzas and shelves and the classy silver accents. But the desk was gone, and so was one of the three big screen monitors. They were in the penthouse now. The other two were sitting on the floor in the corner.

The room looked untouched, except for the dusting, which the cleaning staff did.

Coco and Estavez hadn't had much use for this area, either.

But Miranda's pulse kicked up when she spied a stack of boxes in the corner. Her mother's death certificate had to be in one of them. She hurried over and opened the first lid. There were papers, all right. She shuffled through them, but they were all about real estate deals. Must belong to Mr. P.

The next box held more legal documents, and the last one was shredded papers that somebody must have forgotten to throw in the trash.

With a sigh, Miranda put the lids back on the boxes and shoved everything back in the corner.

She went through the other bedrooms one by one. When she got to the master, she thought her emotions were spent. But when she stepped inside the huge room, she turned to mush.

It was almost as she remembered it, with its soft designer blue walls and cherry-and-plum accents. Gray gauze curtains still hung from the tall arched windows. Overhead the crystal chandelier was still there. She didn't look too closely at the bed, except to notice the comforter had been replaced by a gray and mauve thing.

She was reliving the first time Parker had brought her here. She'd gotten a bite from a baby alligator, of all things, and had passed out. She'd awoken to this room and its irresistible owner. That had been a night for the ages.

And then she noticed the arm chairs in the corner had been replaced by a white bassinet and a matching rocking chair, both with pale blue and pink cushions.

Lullaby time.

Sternly Miranda shook herself. she wasn't here for reminiscing or emoting over the baby's arrival.

She turned to the walk-in closet that had been hers and started digging. Coco's frilly things replaced her spartan wardrobe, cramming every bit of the space. But there were no papers here.

Crossing the room, she stepped into Parker's closet. It seemed even bigger than she recalled, and still had a masculine smell. Estavez's cologne. Like father, like son.

And like father, like son, the rods were packed with designer suits, dress shirts and ties. Built in drawers held polo shirts and accessories. There was a shoe rack on the bottom that held designer dress shoes and brand name athletic shoes.

That was about it.

She was about to go when her gaze rose to an upper shelf, and she spied the corner of gray metal under a blanket.

Standing on tiptoe, she pushed the blanket aside. Under it was a small cash box. With the key in it.

Not very secure.

She pulled it off the shelf, set it on the floor, and sat down beside it. Gingerly she turned the key and opened the lid.

There was a tray with some spare change, a couple of pens, and some small bills. Had Parker left this behind? Or did this box belong to Estavez? With two fingers, she lifted the tray and found more papers. Small ones.

Receipts for jewelry and clothes. Things Parker had bought her at Elegant Ensembles. This box was his, all right. Under the receipts were hospital bills from her stay after Leon's attack in Lake Placid. More for her rehab. She thought of those long, painful months and how close she and Parker had grown then.

He must have paid whatever the Agency's employee insurance hadn't covered.

Well, this was a nice walk down memory lane, but it wasn't getting her anywhere. She was about to put the tray back, when she saw a manila envelope under another jewelry receipt.

She pulled it out, peeked inside, and sucked in a breath.

The title read, "State of Illinois. Division of Vital Statistics." This was it.

"Eureka," she said out loud. She'd found it.

She pulled the document out of the envelope and scanned the details. She could almost smell the dust in the attic where she'd first read the thing.

Cause of death. "Subdural hematoma." "Heart failure." "Fracture of the cervical vertebrae."

She remembered the words of Mrs. Gavinski, her neighbor. "One of the cleaning staff had dropped a wet sponge on the steps. Hilda didn't see it in time. She stepped on it, slipped, and fell down the stairs onto that cold, hard concrete. A whole flight down. She broke her neck and died instantly. But the doctor who declared her dead mentioned heart failure."

Miranda had to take a few deep breaths at the memory of that revelation. But she had what she needed.

This document proved it.

She put everything back in the cash box, put it back on the shelf, and was just about to dig for her phone, when it rang.

It was Aunt Lu. "Well, what did your husband say?"

Her mother's sister sure was pushy. "He's in a meeting. But it doesn't matter. I found the proof you wanted."

"Proof?"

"Yes. I'm holding my mother's death certificate in my hand right now. It clearly states the cause of her death." She read the words aloud.

No response.

"I can send you a copy. Would you like it faxed, emailed, or snail mailed?"

"I already have a copy."

What? "You do?" Then why was Aunt Lu wasting her time?

"Cause of death doesn't tell the whole story," she said in a surly tone. "I would think a hot shot detective would know that."

Miranda put a hand on her hip, wanting to reach through the phone and give her aunt a slap—as disrespectful as that would be.

Then she remembered something. "You told me my mother had a heart attack."

She'd heard it at her mother's funeral, too. She and Parker had gone to Chicago in hopes of finding her daughter. Her mother's heart attack had indicated Hilda Steele might have had a hereditary illness that would make a judge open the adoption records.

She had forced herself to call her aunt then to confirm it.

"That's right. But after you contacted me, I got to thinking. Hilda had always been as healthy as a Clydesdale. It didn't make sense for her heart to give out. So I looked into it. I called the police and they sent me a copy of the death certificate."

The one she had now.

"And then I called the hospital, and one of the staff told me what happened."

Miranda recalled sitting in Mrs. G's claustrophobic, too-warm living room, her little dog in its bed while her former neighbor had explained it to her. Her mother had been working a late shift and she was late delivering her medications. She took a shortcut down a stairwell and didn't see a sponge a cleaning person had accidentally dropped on the stairs. She slipped, fell down to the concrete landing, hit her head, and broke her neck. Some doctor had mentioned heart failure, so that's what they told everyone.

"When I heard that, I had a seismic shift."

"Seismic shift?"

"Why, it was such a shock. That news changed everything I believed about how my sister passed. I knew something wasn't right. I was going to hire a private investigator myself, and then I saw your name in the news, along with your husband's."

Feeling dizzy, Miranda pressed a hand to her forehead. "What are you saying, Aunt Lu?"

"Isn't it obvious? Someone put that sponge there on purpose."

Miranda blinked. She couldn't be serious. "Why would somebody do that?"

Aunt Lu let out a snort. "You know what Hilda was like."

Yeah, she knew. Cold. Stoney. Critical. Humorless. A lot like Aunt Lu. "And so?"

"And so, don't you think she made a few enemies at her job?"

She probably did. But had she made someone mad enough to kill her?

Miranda didn't know what to say. All she knew was that she wasn't enjoying this walk down memory lane. And yet, she'd had the same questions when she'd first learned the truth about her mother's death.

"I'm going to have to talk to Parker about this, Aunt Lu."

"That's what you said before."

"I know but—"

Her phone buzzed with a text. It was Parker, speak of the handsome devil.

"Hold on a minute."

She switched over, read the message—and stopped breathing.

I had to leave the office suddenly. Got a call from a client. I'm in Florida. Be back tonight.

Miranda's head began to swim. Florida? Florida?

She started to tremble with anger as her mind shot back to the morning a couple weeks ago when they'd come back to the Agency after spending time in the North Georgia mountains—and to what she'd seen on Parker's computer screen in his office.

The article on Donavan Santana, complete with a chill-inducing photo of the man.

The article had said the authorities were searching for Santana along the Gulf of Mexico in Alabama. She'd known ever since they'd retired, Parker had been trying to find the man who had caused them so much grief. She'd been doing that herself. Neither of them had exactly been transparent about it, except by accident. But they both knew what the other was doing.

Client, her patootie.

But Florida? Parker hadn't mentioned which town in Florida, but the southern tip of that state was about a hundred miles from the island where Santana had held him prisoner. What in the world was he doing there? Surely he wasn't going back to that island. Whatever he was doing, he was doing it without her. After they'd promised each other—again—there would be no more secrets between them.

She had a good mind to show up and join him whether he wanted her there or not. But she didn't know exactly where he was.

Hah, she thought. Two could play this going-off-on-your-own game.

Her head pounding with rage, she gave her phone a sharp swipe. "Aunt Lu?"

"Yes?"

"Parker's unavailable. I'm going to Chicago to straighten this out myself."

Aunt Lu let out a cough of surprise. "Well, it's about time."

"I'll keep you posted."

She hung up and left the Parker estate without even saying goodbye to Coco.

She hurried back to the penthouse, booked a flight, packed a bag, and headed for Hartsfield-Jackson.

Her temples were still throbbing when the Boeing 717 to O'Hare airport began to zoom down the runway. She hadn't been this angry with Parker in a long, long time.

But as her stomach compressed with the force of the takeoff, deep down inside, in the place where she didn't want to look, she knew what she really felt for him was sheer dread.

CHAPTER FIVE

Wade Parker sped along the Tampa, Florida causeway in his rented Audi, cruising over the final stretch of water as he headed west to the coast.

Squinting through his designer sunglasses, he adjusted the visor.

The sparse rows of palm trees on either side of the road did little to dim the sun's bright reflection off the pavement, or the neighboring vehicles, or the water. The rays were hot and angry.

But not as hot and angry as he was.

His anger was controlled, though. Focused. Not as explosive as he'd expected after the lead he'd received this morning.

Almost two weeks ago, he had found an article in an Alabama newspaper detailing the hunt for the speedboat that had belonged to Donovan Santana—the boat Santana had used to escape the island off Cuba where he'd been holding several hundred people prisoner, including Parker.

Memories of that island, of what that man had done to him, to others, and especially to Miranda had the fire in Parker's gut churning. Santana had been the head of an international crime ring. He was ruthless. He craved more and more power.

He had nearly destroyed the entire country to satisfy his lust.

And the knowledge of the man's true heritage only made the flame inside Parker grow to a feverish pitch.

Parker still couldn't believe he was related to that abomination.

After reading the Alabama newspaper article several times, as soon as he'd had a moment, Parker had contacted the authorities in the Gulf town. To his surprise, he'd discovered a former student was in charge of the investigation there. Graham Chadwick, who was now a senior intelligence specialist with the Coast Guard. Graham had been with the Agency when it was about five years old, and had been one of its finest employees. Parker had fond memories of working with him.

After sharing those memories on the phone, Graham had been forthcoming, but had little to tell Parker that he didn't already know. The rumors about a speedboat washing up on shore were just that. Rumors. In Alabama alone, Graham and his people had thirty-two miles of beachfront and almost a dozen beaches to search, as well as the expanse of the Gulf of Mexico itself, if Santana's boat had capsized out there.

But Graham promised to relay any findings.

Late last week Parker received a call from Graham.

It turned out there had been substance to the rumors. His unit had recovered a boat matching the description of the vessel Santana had used to escape from the island off Cuba. It wasn't a mere speedboat. It was a high-end cruiser with an engine capable of top speeds. Blood had been found inside the cabin. The compartments for equipment and supplies were empty. There had been an identification number on the hull, but it was unregistered.

There was no way to prove the boat belonged to Santana.

But Parker had had an idea.

The boat could have gotten only so far, before Santana would have had to stop for gas. By his calculations, Parker believed Santana must have made it to Tampa. There he refueled and headed out across the Gulf, toward Alabama.

Now the task was to narrow down which of the multitude of docks Santana had used in the Tampa area. Parker and Graham contacted the Criminal Intelligence Unit of the Tampa police department. An investigator began a search of all the possible places Santana might have refueled.

Parker hadn't expected results for a month.

But this morning he had no sooner finished his shower in the penthouse when Graham had called back. The Tampa investigator had found something interesting.

Something he would not release to Parker via email. Something Parker had to see for himself.

Parker made arrangements for the trip immediately and here he was, flying down this causeway, fighting back rage and anticipation.

His phone buzzed.

He pressed the button on the Audi's hands-free screen and winced at the mechanical voice.

Okay. See you then.

Miranda's terse response to the equally terse text message he'd sent her as soon as he'd landed. He could feel the anger in her words, as hot as his own. She had seen the Gulf Shores article on his computer screen two weeks ago. She knew he'd been looking into Santana's disappearance behind her back, just as he knew she was behind his.

She would guess what he was doing.

But he could not tell her about this particular venture. She would want to be involved, and he would not have that.

A little over a month ago, he'd believed she was dead. He had almost lost her twice since then. There would be no more risk-taking. Once Curt Holloway was replaced, Parker was determined to go back into retirement with her, not to go on another adventure.

As soon as he took care of this detail, he would make that happen. If he were lucky, that would be very soon.

As he made his way around the traffic circle, Parker eyed the plethora of sun-and-sand-themed resorts and cafes. Grills and spas crowded the strip of land that housed some of the best beaches in southwestern Florida.

He took an exit, turned left, and made his way to a parking area near one of the marinas.

It wasn't long before he spotted a tall, broad shouldered man with premature gray hair standing next to a government vehicle. His suit was a dark lightweight linen with a matching tie, and he looked to be Parker's own age.

Parker pulled into a nearby space, exited the vehicle, dropped some coins in the parking meter, and approached the man, a hand extended. "You're the intelligence officer I spoke to this morning?"

"John Gutierrez, CIU, Tampa PD." They shook.

"Thank you for including me in your investigation."

"Once Lieutenant Graham Chadwick explained who you were and how you were involved in the incident, we had no other choice."

Parker appreciated the man's commitment. "And the video?"

"Follow me."

They made their way over the wide sidewalk, under the palm trees and past the open seating area of a restaurant grilling hot dogs, to the Harbormaster's Office.

Inside the building was cool, the decor bright and airy, with enough windows to keep an eye on everything that went on in the marina. If you had enough manpower for the more than two hundred slips in the sunny bay. Hence the video surveillance.

Gutierrez led Parker to the second floor and knocked on a door labeled Captain Arnold Wallace.

"Come in," called a gruff voice.

Gutierrez opened the door to a corner office with sparse furnishings and tall windows overlooking the docks below. Diplomas were displayed on the light-colored wall next to a large computer screen. A round mirror was mounted in the corner to give a view of the room from any angle.

A large man sat behind an unadorned desk. He had on a gray striped tie and a gray suit. His head was shaved, but he appeared to be younger than Gutierrez.

As Parker and Gutierrez approached, Wallace stuck out a meaty hand. "Glad to meet you, Mr. Parker. I've been working with Gutierrez here, and I must say, this case is rather alarming. Please, have a seat."

Parker settled into a cushioned guest chair while Gutierrez took the other one. "I'd say that's an understatement, Captain."

"I suppose it is. I can't believe what I saw on this footage. I have to say, I'm grateful to Gutierrez and his team for digging it up."

Meaning his people had missed it. "Why don't you show me what you have."

"Of course. I have Lieutenant Chadwick on speaker on the computer. He'll be watching the video at the same time."

Wallace pressed a button and Graham's intense face appeared on the screen. Like the others, he was in the requisite suit-and-tie, and his dark hair was a military buzz cut.

"Good afternoon, Graham."

"Good afternoon, Mr. Parker. Gentlemen. I hope this is good. I wouldn't want to waste this man's time."

"It's definitely not a waste of time." Captain Wallace turned to his laptop, fiddled with the keys awhile, and paused, as if he wasn't sure what the next step was. Then he discovered the correct key and pressed it.

An image appeared on the screen on the wall.

The surveillance camera had been mounted on a building along the dock, giving them a close perspective of a slice of the area. The weathered gray boards of the pier came into view, and waves rippled in the blue water of the bay. Two rows of sailboats, power riders, and other recreational crafts lined either side of the marina.

The faint sound of a motor came through the speakers, and gradually, a white vessel appeared, puttering through the other boats. It was moving in reverse, its stern heading slowly for the dock and the fuel pump that stood on it. When the cruiser reached the dock, it stopped, the engine was turned off, and a young man emerged.

Parker recognized him instantly.

He wasn't wearing a lab coat now. He was in a drab gray T-shirt, khaki shorts, and sneakers. But the sandy curls parted down the middle of his head and the thick rimmed glasses were unmistakable.

The boy opened the boat's fuel cap, took the nozzle from the pump, and began to fill the vessel.

This was something, but not enough.

Suddenly a man's face appeared in a rear window of the boat. "Ninety percent, maximum," he grunted.

"Yes, I remember," the boy said nervously.

Parker felt as if he had been punched in the gut. "Stop the video."

Captain Wallace pressed a key, and the image froze.

Parker shot to his feet and went to the screen to examine it more closely. But he didn't need to. "That's him," he told the officers, pointing to the face in the rear window. "That's Donovan Santana. And I recognize the boy with him. His name is Phineas. Santana called him his biopharmaceutical researcher. I believe he's the adolescent genius who created the mind control drug Santana used on his victims. The substance they called the Elixir."

There was a long silence in the room as the two men processed that information. They already knew those details from the statements Parker had given the authorities the day he and the other prisoners were rescued.

"We have a little more," Wallace said at last, and pressed another key.

The video continued.

The boy shut off the pump, returned the nozzle, and went to the counter to pay. He paid with cash so there would be no way to trace the transaction. But the security camera had captured the hull of the boat where the identification number had been painted.

Wallace stopped the video again.

Parker read the letters and number combination aloud. It was the same as the boat that had been abandoned in Gulf Shores.

That had indeed been Santana's vessel.

"My."

Wallace pressed a button, and Graham's face reappeared, looking even more intense.

"We've confirmed the HIN, Graham." Parker told him. "The cabin cruiser you discovered did in fact belong to Santana."

"Yes, I see that." Graham let out a long sigh and ran a hand across his face. "Good to know, but I'm afraid the trail here has gone cold."

"What do you mean?"

"I mean there's no trace of Donovan Santana other than that boat. Nothing in the local hotels. Nothing in the bus stations or taxi companies. We don't know what happened to him. Or that boy."

Were they using all their resources? Surely Santana and that boy had left some trace of themselves somewhere. Parker didn't ask. He didn't want to insult his former student. He knew he was doing his best, but he wanted to take a look at what they had found himself.

That would mean a trip to Alabama. What was he going to tell Miranda? It wouldn't be easy to keep her from following him down here. He'd think of something. He had to.

If Donovan Santana was still out there, sooner or later, he would come after them again. He had to be stopped.

Parker would find him first.

"I'll be in Gulf Shores in a couple of hours," he told Graham.

Then he said goodbye to the officers and headed back to the parking lot.

Reaching for his phone, he climbed into the Audi and began to make the travel arrangements.

And to think of what to say to Miranda.

CHAPTER SIX

Miranda tipped the bellhop and stepped into the luxury hotel suite she'd booked in Oak Park, Illinois.

It was nice.

Plush leather couches and chairs, glass-top tables, a kitchenette loaded with granite and stainless steel. Yeah, nice.

It had been her anger at Parker that had made her pick the priciest hotel in town—as well as rent the white Tesla Model S with matching interior and full glass roof that she'd driven from the airport—and put them all on her Agency credit card.

Why not? Isn't that what Parker would have done? If he were here.

But no, he was somewhere in Florida with a "client."

Ha.

That Ludicrous Mode was something else. Zero-to-sixty in a heartbeat. What a rush.

But she wasn't here to joyride or to gloat. She had to prove to Aunt Lu that her mother's death was an accident, and get that pesky woman off her back.

Grabbing her laptop case, she set up on the desk facing the window and settled into the cushy high back chair. Next to the lamp, she found a basket of amenities. She took a minute to sift through it. Sodas, chocolates, a bottle of water, brochures for Frank Lloyd Wright's studio and Hemingway's birthplace. Like she'd told herself. Nice. There was also a newspaper tucked in among the brochures.

Maybe she'd order room service for lunch, she thought as she opened the paper and scanned the front page. Her shoulders stiffened and her breath caught.

"Serial Killer Strikes Again."

There had been another victim.

Miranda's stomach tensed as she read Detective Templeton's statement to the reporter. The police had confirmed the case in Kenwood had been the work of the same killer. The victim found in Hyde Park—the one Templeton had asked for her help on—had been the second. There had been another two weeks ago, and a fourth they found yesterday.

Definitely the work of a serial killer. A busy one.

Miranda folded the paper and put it in the trash basket. No lunch for her now.

Her mind raced as she stared at her blank laptop screen. Four young women dead. All blond. All college students.

The need to help, to do something rose up in her. Her calling. Her destiny. She had the sudden urge to call Templeton.

Maybe she and Parker shouldn't have turned her down.

No. They were retired. Or trying to be. And besides, that wasn't why she'd come here. She had to focus on her mother.

It would be quick and easy. Talk to some people at the hospital, find some old records, call Aunt Lu, done. She might not even have to spend the night in this place.

She turned on the laptop, opened a search engine, and stalled.

She didn't even remember which hospital her mother had worked in. That was how close they'd been.

C'mon, she thought. What did her mother tell her every night when she went out the door?

Mostly she left a note with abbreviated instructions on how to cook whatever she'd left in the fridge for dinner. That was when Miranda had started eating dinner from a bag of tortilla chips.

Wait. She reached for her laptop case and pulled the death certificate out of a pocket.

There it was. Suburban General Hospital.

Okay. She returned to her keyboard, typed in the name, and found their website.

Huge place. They'd recently expanded for the second time in a decade and built another new wing and a new Emergency Unit.

She hunted around and found a photo of the CEO.

Bryant Williamson. Nice looking young man in a dark blue suit and tie. He had closely cropped brown hair, friendly blue eyes, straight teeth, and a warm smile meant to exude compassion. Lots of letters after his name.

"We serve with care," his bio began. Then it went on to tout his lengthy experience in healthcare administration and not-for-profit organizations. Dude must be older than he looked. But his curriculum vitae was impressive. Said he had a good working relationship with IDPH, the Illinois Department of Public Health, the organization that oversaw all hospitals.

Interesting.

Miranda tapped her fingers on the table.

Should she go straight to the head honcho? She thought of Parker's reaction when Mrs. G told them about her mother's accidental fall down the hospital staircase and why everyone decided to say she'd had a heart attack.

He'd said it was a cover-up, implying negligence.

If she went barging into the director's office, demanding to know what had happened to her mother, they'd clam up for sure. They'd think she was there for a lawsuit.

They'd kick her out, and she'd never get the proof she needed for Aunt Lu.

Better to take a subtle approach. Ask around, see who knew who and what.

Closing her laptop, she got to her feet, and went to the bathroom to check herself in the full length mirror.

She was in the clothes she'd worn to work this morning.

Navy slacks, pinstripe jacket, white top, dark dress pumps. She ran her fingers through her hair to straighten it as best she could.

It would do.

Just a professional enough look to get some pertinent information out of somebody. Grabbing her phone and a small bag, she felt her hopes rising. She might even be able to catch the nine o'clock flight back home.

In time to have it out with Parker.

CHAPTER SEVEN

As she headed east to North Austin in her rented Tesla, Miranda scanned the still vaguely familiar buildings. Old memories began to hit her.

Oak Park was fancy to the north, but Miranda had grown up in the not-so-ritzy area closer to the city. The house she'd lived in with Leon wasn't far away. Neither was the one she'd grown up in.

Thankfully, she'd be sticking to the north side for this trip. Still she remembered these streets. The shops, the sidewalks. She passed a skate park, and as she slowed for a traffic light, she had a flashback of herself sitting on a swing back there late at night.

She must have been in seventh grade. Her mother had been at work when Miranda had come home from school that day. Deciding she didn't like the dried out meatloaf her mother had left her for dinner, she'd called a friend, and they went to a fast food place within walking distance. Miranda had paid for it with her allowance money.

She'd forgotten her mother had given her an allowance. It wasn't much, but that night Miranda had blown her whole stash on burgers and fries and milkshakes. She'd been lonely and she was trying to buy friends.

There had been some older boys there, and the two girls had flirted with them. Miranda had just become interested in boys. It was long before Leon.

Then the store closed, and the manager kicked them out.

She couldn't remember who'd suggested going to the park, but she recalled walking there, and she could still hear the squeals and laughter as the older boys pushed her and her friend on the swings.

And then her friend remembered she had homework, and everyone left—and Miranda sat there alone on the swing, afraid to go home.

She wasn't sure what time it was or when her mother would be home, but all she could think of was her waiting for her with her angry face and her belt.

She should have gone home and faced the music.

Instead, maybe an hour later, her mother had pulled up in her old clunky car and chugged into the park and across the grass.

"Miranda," she'd barked in her gruff voice. "What in the world are you doing here?"

"Having fun?" Miranda had shrugged.

Eyes blazing, her mother grabbed her by the arm. "When will you learn that life isn't fun? It's hard and painful. It isn't a party." She dragged her to the car and shoved her into the backseat.

The belt was waiting when they got home. Miranda thought she'd drawn blood that time. Then her mother locked her in her room and didn't let her out for two days. She'd missed some school and had to make it up. The dry meatloaf had tasted pretty good after that.

That was when, she remembered now, she started to look for a way to escape.

A horn blared behind her and she jumped. The light had turned green.

"Okay," she muttered, taking her foot off the brake.

Why was she here in Oak Park again?

Oh, yeah. To get Aunt Lu off her back.

Shaking off the bad feelings from the past, she made her turn, and blasted through traffic in the Tesla.

CHAPTER EIGHT

It didn't take long to get to Suburban General, and she decided to check out the exterior first.

Miranda rolled through the covered drive and up to the sleek new emergency entrance. There she followed the signs to the covered drive-up of the brand new main entrance, then cruised around the parking lot until she found a spot in visitor parking.

The main entrance was her best bet to gain access, she decided. So she got out, locked the Tesla, and plodded across the pavement, passing an elderly couple and a large, disgruntled looking man in the lot.

The double glass doors whisked open as she approached, and when she was past them, Miranda found herself in a tall open space with a fancy brick sculpture thing that went all the way up to the upper floors.

Around her was glossy white tile and pale wood forming a circular shape. Here and there landscapes and openings to hallways broke the monotony of the circle.

A family sat in a comfortable looking seating area. A hospitality suite was behind them. Looked more like a five-star hotel than a hospital.

In the middle of the space stood a directory covered in shiny blue glass. Miranda walked over and studied the white lettering.

Radiology, Oncology, Neuroscience. Emergency.

She tapped her foot. All she wanted was to talk to a couple of people who knew her mother way back when.

Glancing back at the front desk, she decided that was her only option. She strolled over to where a woman sat behind the paneling.

"Can I help you?" she smiled at Miranda as she approached.

The woman was wearing a silky mauve print jacket accented with a gold chain. Her thick red-brown hair hung around her face in loose curls.

Miranda smiled back at her. "I think you might."

"Are you here to see a patient?" Her voice was warm and friendly.

"Uh…" Saying she wanted to talk to someone who knew Hilda Steele seventeen years ago would be lame, and she didn't want to mention the accident.

Miranda cleared her throat. "Actually, I'm here to see my mother. She works here."

The friendly look on the woman's face turned to a wary frown. "Oh. What department is she in?"

"Uh…" if Miranda couldn't remember the name of the hospital, she sure wasn't going to recall the department her mother worked in. She wasn't even sure her mother had ever told her. She thought of the words on the directory. "Radiology maybe? I'm not sure. Could you just look her up?" Miranda gestured to the computer screen on the desk.

The woman's frown turned to a look of deeper suspicion. She was responsible not only for directing people to the right place, but for keeping the unwanted out of places they weren't supposed to go.

She shifted her weight as if she were sitting on peanuts. "I'm sorry. You'd have to see someone in HR for that information."

She probably didn't have access to seventeen-year-old records, anyway.

Miranda forced another smile for the woman. "Okay. Where do I find HR?"

"Human Resources is on the second floor, but it would be better to call first." As in, please go away.

Miranda widened her fake smile. "Since I'm already here, why don't you just point me in the right direction."

"I'm sorry, but—"

"Julia?" called a voice from somewhere in the back.

The woman at the desk held up a finger. "One moment."

Looking nervous, she rose and hurried toward an office behind her where someone was sitting at another desk behind a glass partition.

"Never mind," Miranda muttered under her breath as she dropped the smile. "I'll find it myself."

And hoping the friendly lady and her boss weren't calling Security, she scooted across the glossy floor and down an aisle marked "Elevators."

CHAPTER NINE

After wandering the halls on the second floor pretending to know where she was going for what seemed like half an hour, Miranda finally found the HR department.

Opening the tall paneled door, she spotted another gatekeeper at a pale marble desk. Overhead a modern style lamp spilled soft light over the desk, giving it an ethereal glow.

Like you were about to meet St. Peter and had better say the right words, or he wouldn't let you in.

St. Peter, in this case, was a woman with sleek black hair cut to her chin line, who was dressed in a black-and-white power suit. Her back was measuring-rod straight, and it grew even straighter as Miranda approached.

Her thin-lipped smile matched her posture, and her eyes bore into Miranda through chic tortoise shell glasses. "I'm sorry, ma'am," she said in an authoritative voice before Miranda got to her desk. "We don't have any openings at the moment. But you can apply online."

Sounded like a real friendly place to work.

"I'm not here about an opening," Miranda said, matching the woman's tone. She'd spent her wandering time coming up with a better story. "I'm inquiring about a job reference."

"A job reference?"

"Someone who applied with us. I'm checking on the records for one of your former employees."

St. Peter narrowed an eye. "You could have called for that information."

Thinking fast, Miranda put on an irritated scowl. "I did call. I was on hold for forty minutes. My time is valuable."

St. Peter's brow rose. "Then why did you tell Julia at the front desk that you were looking for your mother?"

Miranda knew that snitch would rat on her. Then she thought of the CEO's bio. "I was checking up on your procedures. We like to do that from time to time at the IDPH."

According to that bio, the Illinois Department of Public Health oversaw all hospitals. In other words, she now had clout. Or was pretending to.

Now both of St. Peter's brows rose. For a long moment, she stared at her with an expression that said she wasn't sure Miranda was telling the truth, but didn't want to risk offending her if she was.

At last, drawing in a breath, she turned to her computer. "When did this employee work here?"

"Seventeen years ago."

Her lips twisted with frustration. "I'm sorry, ma'am, I'm afraid we don't keep records that long."

"Aren't you required to keep them indefinitely?" Miranda seemed to remember from her IIT training that it was a long time. She couldn't recall exactly how long.

"You misunderstood me. We don't keep records online beyond five years. They're in the archives."

"And where can I find these archives?"

"Records Retention is in the basement of the older section. Just follow this map." Now smiling sweetly, she tapped a sticker on her desk.

Miranda looked down and saw it was a QR code. My, aren't we state-of-the-art.

Wondering if she'd disintegrate in place and be transported somewhere if she used it, she took out her phone, snapped a photo of the code, and the map appeared on her screen.

Records Retention was in room B-12. Like the vitamin.

It looked like it was a long way away.

But she was making progress. She hoped.

"Thanks so much," she told the woman.

And then she turned on her heel and headed back out to the elevators.

CHAPTER TEN

The trek to the Records Retention department in the old building was so long and convoluted, Miranda thought a walk to the Indiana dunes would have been quicker.

First, she had to go all the way around the perimeter to the opposite side of the new building. Then she had to cross a long glass bridge spanning both structures, where she could see the tops of cars passing beneath her feet. Finally she reached the hospital's old section.

It was definitely ancient.

Green cinder block walls, old linoleum, musty smells. Miranda wondered if her mother had worked in this area, though she still didn't have a clue which department she had been assigned to.

Glancing down at her map, she learned this floor had once been the Neurosurgery unit and was now used for research projects and teaching. She squinted at the labels.

Crap. She was on the third floor, and she needed to go to the basement. This map was worthless.

Summoning another dose of willpower, she walked around a bit, following what she thought was the exterior hallway. But she couldn't find the elevator. Did this section even have one?

She hadn't seen many hospital personnel in the area, but just now she heard a door open somewhere. Voices echoed in the hallway.

Rounding the curve of a wall, two young men in blue scrubs appeared. They looked like interns, and they were engrossed in a technical conversation.

"Have you read Dr. Newman's article on the corpus callosum?" said the one on the left.

The one on the right nodded with excitement. "Yes, it was fascinating."

"His research could lead to significant breakthroughs."

"I agree. Let's discuss it over a bite to eat. We missed lunch, and I hear they're serving beef stew today."

"Hmm. The cafeteria's beef stew is almost palatable."

As they chuckled over the comment, Miranda stepped in front of them, blocking their path. "Excuse me. I'm looking for room B-12. Can you help me out?"

The men stared at her as if in shock.

The one on the left had a blond buzzcut, the one on the right had dark hair combed over his forehead. Both had smooth faces and skinny bodies. Both had probably been in high school when her mother worked here.

No use asking if they'd known her.

The dark haired one on the right cocked his head. "Are you a new employee?"

"Sort of," she fibbed. "HR sent me to Records Retention." That much was true.

He shook his head. "I'm sorry. I'm not familiar with that department."

His cohort tapped his shoulder. "We need to get going before they run out of stew."

The dark haired one gave her a quick grin. "Why don't you try the Information Desk at the front."

The pair started to hurry off.

"Can you tell me where the elevator is?"

The dark haired guy pointed over his shoulder. "Around that corner."

And they disappeared down the hall she'd just come from.

Miranda turned toward the corner he'd indicated. She'd been going the wrong way. So much for the digital map.

She stood there, hesitating.

Everyone she'd seen at this hospital so far seemed pretty young. No one who worked here now would have known her mother.

Despair began to tug at her heart. What was she trying to accomplish? It was pointless, wasn't it? Digging up the past? She should just tell Aunt Lu the hospital records confirmed the story of her mother's death and be done with it. Someone left a sponge on the stairs, and her mother slipped on it and took a fatal tumble down the hard concrete steps.

And died.

Tragic, but it was over and done with.

And then a sick feeling stirred in the pit of her stomach. She thought about when Mrs. G had told her that story. She thought about Parker saying the hospital was negligent. She'd had the same feeling then, but she'd ignored it. Buried it. Refused to acknowledge it.

But now Aunt Lu and this trip to Suburban General Hospital had dredged it up again.

The details of Mrs. G's story had never quite set right with her. Not that Mrs. G was lying. She was just repeating what she'd heard. But something felt off about it.

What had really happened to her mother? Didn't she want to know for sure?

She did, Miranda decided.

Straightening her shoulders, she headed around the corner and found the elevators.

And again she came to a halt.

On the wall beside a cubby hole a few feet away was a sign of a stick figure descending a jagged line. Stairs.

Icy fingers began to work their way up Miranda's spine.

Crossing the hall to the recess, she opened the heavy door, stepped onto the landing, and leaned over the cold iron rail to stare at the hard concrete stairs and the landing below.

She felt a pressure in her chest. Suddenly it was hard to breathe.

Was this where her mother died?

Heart pounding, she raced down the steps and peered down at the hard concrete surface of the lower landing.

Then she bent down and ran her hand over it. Just the normal gritty feel of cement.

She didn't see any blood stains, but those would have worn away after seventeen years. If this was even the right stairwell. There were probably a few in this place.

She shook herself. This wasn't getting her anywhere.

Rising, she took a deep breath and steadied herself. Better go back up or she might get lost again.

With a new surge of determination, she headed up the stairs and made her way to the elevator and down to Records Retention on the lowest level.

CHAPTER ELEVEN

A flickering fluorescent light overhead cast eerie shadows over faded green cinder brick walls as Miranda moved down a corridor that seemed endless.

There was no one down here. The air was dry and a little too warm, and except for the snapping light, it was silent.

Kinda creepy.

She wondered if the morgue was down here. Why not store dead bodies next to old dead records?

It seemed as if Miranda had walked a mile before she found room B-12, but at last a tarnished sign on a plain gray door told her she was in the right place.

Records Retention.

She opened the door and stepped inside.

What?

Miranda found herself facing a row of head-high black filing cabinets. The back of them. The musty smell of old papers was in the air.

Turning, she saw the cabinets formed an aisle with the wall.

Might as well see where it went.

Before she did, she twisted the knob of the door she'd come through, just to make sure it hadn't locked behind her.

The knob still turned.

Exhaling her relief, she made her way down the makeshift row, and as she reached the end of it, she heard a clicking sound. Typing. On a loud keyboard.

Daring to poke her head around the last filing cabinet, Miranda saw more rows of black cabinets beyond this one, reaching all the way to the back.

Across from the cabinets was an area about the space of three aisles. On the other side were rows of tall shelves filled with bankers boxes. Reminded Miranda of an evidence room.

Not a window in sight.

In the middle of the center space, sat a clunky old metal desk like the ones she'd seen at police stations with low budgets.

At the desk sat a woman working on the computer with the noisy keyboard. She looked to be in her early forties. She wore dark-rimmed half glasses, had on jeans and a plaid green shirt, and had her ash brown hair caught up in a messy bun. Miranda thought she saw a pen sticking out of it.

The woman stopped typing for a moment, squinted at her computer screen, and took the pen out of her hair to scratch her head.

Forty-something nerdy type?

Time to play inspector from the IDPH again.

Miranda inhaled, straightened her jacket, and came around the filing cabinet with as authoritative a stride as she could muster.

She glanced down at the nameplate on the desk.

"Ms. Jaworski?"

The woman startled and squinted up at Miranda over the top of her glasses. "That's me," she said in a voice that sounded like a growling bulldog. "How did you get in here?"

Miranda pointed toward the filing cabinets. "Through the door."

Ms. Jaworski scowled. "That's the back door. The front door is right there." She pointed behind Miranda.

Miranda turned her head. Sure enough, there was another door that looked like the main entrance.

She turned back. "It wasn't clearly marked. You should fix that."

Ms. Jaworski curled a lip. "We'll get right on that. So you're the lady from IDPH?"

Again she'd been ratted out by the HR guard dog. They sure had a speedy grapevine here.

Might as well go with it. "Then you know why I'm here."

The woman glared at her over her half glasses. "I assure you we comply with all regulations under federal and state law."

Her tone said if Miranda was from IDPH, she was Lady Gaga.

"Actually, I'm checking a reference of a former employee."

Ms. Jaworski twisted her lips as if that was the lamest lie she'd ever heard. But she turned to her keyboard. "Name."

Now Miranda was getting somewhere. "Hilda Steele."

"And she worked here seventeen years ago?"

The grapevine was specific as well as speedy.

"That's right."

The woman turned to her computer, and the clicky-typing sound started up again.

Then it stopped and she squinted at her screen. "Oh," she said, and clicked something. "Uh, there she is. Hmm."

Her frown deepened as she leaned in toward the screen.

Miranda's stomach tensed. "Does it say what department she worked in?"

Ms. Jaworski glared at her as if she had turned into a space monster. She got to her feet. "Excuse me."

And she scampered off into the shelves.

What in the world was on that computer? Miranda wasn't leaving until she found out. She hurried around the desk and leaned down to have a look.

It was a computer form.

A light blue background with a lot of fields that had been filled in.

Basic information. Name, address, phone number, social. Her mother's application. Her W4. Sheesh, her pay had been low.

Started off as a cleaning person and worked her way up to LPN. She worked in Neurosurgery. What? Her mother had worked with brain surgeons? Miranda was stunned. The text said her mother had been taking classes and was just about to become a full-fledged RN. She was at the top of her class.

And then Miranda saw the next words.

"Termination date."

Miranda flinched. Her memory banks knew that date. It was the day her mother died. Now there was a double entendre.

And there it was.

"Action Reason. Death."

There was another button marked Confidential. Miranda clicked it. A document opened. Its title took Miranda's breath.

"Inquiry into the Hilda Steele Case."

The hospital had done an inquiry? Why didn't she know that? Still, that document would give her the answers she was looking for.

There was a print button.

She looked around and spotted the printer along the back wall.

She turned back to the screen and looked at the top bar. Thirty-two pages.

Could she get it done before Ms. Sunshine came back?

She was just about to reach for the mouse when she heard voices coming from the shelving units.

"This is highly irregular," said a booming male voice. "It will have to be dealt with immediately."

Uh oh. Busted again. Crap.

Memorizing the report's number, she closed the document, scooted around the desk, and hurried to the aisle behind the filing cabinets where she'd come in.

She'd just put her hand on the knob when the booming voice rang out behind her.

"Hold it right there, Miss."

She turned around and saw Jaworski and her bulky boss behind her. They were both scowling.

Bracing herself, Miranda folded her arms. She'd better come up with something good now.

She was considering threatening to write them up when the boss man opened his mouth and growled, "Our CEO would like to speak with you."

CHAPTER TWELVE

Fifteen minutes later Miranda was sitting in a cushy teal-colored chair in a bright corner office on the fourth floor of the new wing.

Across from her Bryant Williamson, CEO of Suburban General, sat behind a walnut executive desk.

Dressed in his typical CEO suit, he looked larger than his picture on the hospital website and older. By at least a decade. His closely cropped brown hair had grown out and turned gray, but his eyes were still just as blue, and his teeth were just as white and straight. Or so she assumed.

He wasn't smiling just now.

Stacks of papers were piled neatly on the desk. A computer sat off to the side. A stethoscope Williamson probably only used for show lay next to it. Diplomas and awards hung in wooden frames behind him on a space set between two large windows.

Studying her, he steepled his hands. "Well, I'd say we've established you're not from IDPH, Ms.—"

Miranda turned her head to gaze at a photo of the Frank Lloyd Wright house mounted near another large window and put on a casual air. "Have we?"

Looking annoyed, Williamson cleared his throat. "Ms. Jaworski didn't appreciate your snooping on her computer."

Feeling like a misbehaving student who'd been sent to the principal's office, Miranda shrugged.

After a long silence Williamson spoke. "Do you want to tell me why you're so interested in Hilda Steele?" His voice was gentle and had a bit of resignation in it.

His tone surprised her. And it got to her. Might as well tell the truth.

Miranda turned her head back and looked Williamson in the eye. "I'm her daughter."

Williamson drew in a slow breath through his nostrils. Not the answer he was expecting. "I—I'm sorry for your loss, Ms. Steele, is it?"

Again, Miranda was surprised by that remark. The compassion exuding from his website photo apparently was genuine.

Most people in the medical profession were compassionate. Miranda respected them for that. She'd been under their care too many times not to. Especially Dr. Talbot, Parker's best friend back in Atlanta, whom she thought the world of.

But this case was a little different from a broken bone or a gunshot wound.

Or even a routine check-up.

Suddenly Williamson sat up, leaned across the desk, and peered at her. "You're *Miranda* Steele, aren't you?"

Uh oh.

Miranda raised her palms. "That's me."

"I saw you on the news. You solved the murder of that attorney a few weeks ago."

The Quinton Prescott case. "Correct again."

Looking very uncomfortable, the CEO reached for what looked like a bound report. "I assure you, Ms. Steele, you won't find anything to investigate in here."

Miranda's gaze went to the report. "What is that?"

"Why, it's the inquiry you were looking at on Ms. Jaworski's computer."

It was?

"She insists it's confidential and should only be released to authorized personnel, but I'm overriding her on this one." To Miranda's shock, Williamson rose, came around the desk, and put the document in her hand.

Stunned, she stared down at the plastic bound thirty-two page report. That easy, huh? She should have followed her instincts and come to the CEO in the first place.

"And this explains what happened to my mother?"

"It's a comprehensive report of our internal investigation."

"Can I keep it?"

He nodded. "It's your copy."

Not knowing what to say, Miranda got to her feet. "Thanks."

With another compassionate smile, Williamson extended a hand. "I hope you find what you're looking for in it."

Miranda shook with him. "Me, too."

But as she gazed into his kind blue eyes, she caught a strange flicker in them that made her stomach tighten. Like maybe he was regretting giving her that report. Like maybe he was a little worried about what she was about to read in there. Like maybe he was hiding something he hoped Miranda wouldn't find out about.

Or maybe she was reading that into his expression. She couldn't tell.

But if this compassionate-appearing CEO was keeping something under wraps, she was going to find out what it was.

He could bet his stethoscope on that.

CHAPTER THIRTEEN

Parker stood on the shore in his suit, staring out at the water of the gulf, his dress shoes sinking into the sugar-white sand of Gulf Shores, Alabama. The waves were calm, the air muggy and smelling of salt. Fishing boats dotted the blue-green expanse.

As he turned his head to focus on the reason for his visit here, Parker's gut went sour. His jaw clenched as he studied the sight.

A thirty-four-foot pearl-white whale of a boat, reclined on the white sand like a sleepy sunbather. Crime scene tape stretched around the boat forming a perimeter of several yards. The yellow plastic fluttered in the light breeze as carelessly as if the thing were a tourist attraction. The whole spectacle was offensive.

Still, Parker longed to go inside the cabin.

He imagined finding Santana in there, taking him by surprise, and finishing him off with his bare fists.

It was a fantasy that would not come true here and now, of course. Santana was long gone. But Parker would indulge it at some point. Or some version of it.

Right now the reality was that the cabin had already been combed by the local authorities, and the evidence had been taken to the police station, so there was little reason to go beyond the tape.

Besides, he didn't dare disturb the sand.

Nonetheless, he had to fight down the memories, the anger of his last encounter with the man. And the fresh vision of him on the security footage Parker had seen a few hours ago in Tampa. He was fighting so hard, he barely heard Graham's voice just behind him.

"The hull was damaged near the bow."

Parker came out of his revenge reverie and peered at the front of the boat where the fiberglass had been gouged by rocks. He nodded. "Indicating Santana ran the boat aground on purpose."

"Yes."

"And that this was his destination."

"Correct," Graham agreed. "The boat wasn't anchored."

A grunt of disgust came from Graham's side. "Santana probably hoped the boat would wash back out into the gulf. And that we wouldn't find it. But we did. The maintenance crew was the first to report the cruiser."

This was spoken in a light coastal accent by Sergeant A.J. Kessling of the Gulf Shores Police Department, who had accompanied Parker and Graham to the crime scene. Kessling and his people were assisting in the hunt for Santana.

The one that had gone nowhere.

Maintenance crew. The workers responsible for clearing the beach of debris left by nature and sunbathers, as well as smoothing the sand.

Parker turned to Kessling. "If Santana was heading here from where he fueled in Tampa, that boat must have sat there for a month. Why didn't the crew spot it earlier?"

Kessling rocked back on his heels. "This beach doesn't see much activity until April. The first crew came out last week and found it. That was when we called in the Coast Guard and Lieutenant Chadwick got involved with the investigation."

Parker nodded, recalling the vast area Graham and his team had covered in their search. "Did the maintenance crew destroy any footprints?"

"We've kept people away from the scene as best we could, Mr Parker." Sergeant Kessling drew in a breath through his nose.

Kessling was on the thin side and stood a few inches shorter than Graham, who was just under Parker's height. He had a narrow face, a straight nose, and large ears under his police cap. A large Adam's apple bobbed over the neckline of his uniform, giving Parker the impression that he didn't care for another investigator getting involved with this manhunt.

However, since Graham had summarized Parker's recent experience with Santana when he introduced him to Kessling, Parker could see respect battling annoyance in the sergeant's expression.

"I have to admit the sand has been contaminated with footprints of tourists and curiosity-seekers since the discovery."

Parker scanned the myriad of indentations in the surface surrounding the boat. Turning, he saw some of them led across the sand to a developed piece of land about a quarter mile away.

"Our theory is that Santana made his way over to Gulf Hills, the residential community over there," Kessling said.

"In fact," Graham continued in a tone as intense as his face, "one of the maintenance workers told us he spotted two pairs of footprints going right up to the edge of the pavement of that piece of property. After what we saw on that video from Tampa earlier, that makes sense."

"The man and the boy." Kessling had been apprised of what they had discovered on the video in Tampa a few hours ago.

Parker narrowed his eyes as he stared at the sandy path to the homes in the distance. "Someone picked him up there."

"He may have befriended a tourist and hitched a ride."

"Or jacked a car," Kessling said.

Parker turned to the man. "Have there been any reports of carjackings recently?"

"Not in the timeframe we're looking at, sir."

Parker shook his head. "Santana has criminal connections all over the country. I'd say he contacted someone and had that person pick him and Phineas up."

"Which means he could have gone anywhere from there." Graham said. "Most likely out of the country."

"Or he could be right here under your noses."

Kessling grimaced at that idea. "As I mentioned, we're re-canvassing the area. We've also put Santana's photo in the local media, asking for information. We've received a few calls."

Nothing worth following. Parker had already been through them with Graham. But it would be good to go over all the information the authorities had gathered.

He hadn't meant to be short with the man. He and his team were doing their best.

He mustered up his most charming smile. "I appreciate that, Sergeant. Let's head back to the station, if you don't mind. I'd like to see what you have."

Kessling's brow rose, but he nodded. "Certainly, sir."

CHAPTER FOURTEEN

The Gulf Shores police station was a simple flat one-story building with the beige brick typical of government structures.

It sat across the street from a row of modest homes making up what appeared to be a quiet middle class neighborhood. A reasonable assumption based on the location.

Parker pulled his second rental of the day into a spot and waited for Graham and Kessling to arrive. When they did, silently he followed them inside.

The interior of the station was as predictable as its exterior. Gray-green paint, dated linoleum floors, a few wanted posters mounted neatly to the walls next to local fundraising notices. The cool air was refreshing, and its antiseptic scent told Parker the floors had been recently mopped.

His escorts led him to a large room in the back where evidence was stored. Off to the side of the shelving and cages was a smaller room with the typical police station metal-and-hard-plastic chairs arranged around a plain industrial style table.

A large evidence box sat in the middle of the table surrounded by notepads, pens, plastic gloves, and water bottles.

Kessling gestured to the box. "Since we knew you were coming, Mr. Parker, I had what we've collected pulled." He sounded sincere.

"I appreciate that."

"Have a seat."

As Parker settled into the chair across from the door, Kessling opened the box and took out a stack of folders.

He set the stack next to the box and handed Parker the first folder. "Transcripts of the tips from callers."

Parker opened the file and scanned the neatly typed notes. There was the usual hyperbole, as well as statements claiming the picture of the suspect shown on TV "looked just like my uncle, or my neighbor, or my ex." Little did they know it was Parker who Santana looked like.

He put down the papers and closed the file. "Nothing of substance here."

Graham scowled in frustration. "No, not yet. Kessling is doing another press conference tonight."

Nodding, Parker reached for the next file. It held photos of the beach they had just come from. He took them out and studied them one by one.

Most were the barefoot prints belonging to the locals and tourists Kessling had mentioned. Parker doubted Santana had removed his shoes to cross the sand. In addition, there were prints of various brands of athletic shoes, flip-flops, ladies' beachwear. But the next photo was the one that caught Parker's attention.

It was a closeup of the unmistakable outline of a dress shoe in the sand. A ruler indicated the size was definitely that of a man's shoe, a little larger than the size Parker wore.

Few people would wear dress shoes on the beach.

The next photo was taken farther back and showed the prints of athletic shoes beside the dress shoes.

Phineas.

Parker squinted at the image carefully. "The spacing between the indentations indicates they were walking rather than running."

"We noticed that, too." Graham said.

Parker peered at the dress shoe prints. "There seems to be more pressure on the right forefoot." He turned the photo lengthwise. "The angle of the right foot is odd, as well. He was limping."

"That was our impression."

A limp? It made sense. Santana must have injured his leg when he fell from the spiral staircase in the bunker. That fall should have killed him, but the evil in the man gave him an uncanny resilience.

Or so Parker believed.

He picked up the last photo. It was a longer shot of the sand and the two pairs of footprints, the dress and athletic shoes, leading up to a stretch of pavement that belonged to Gulf Hills.

"Tell me more about this area."

Kessling opened another folder and took out a map of the area, with its spider-like stretches of beach.

He tapped a finger on the spot in question.

"This section is what we saw from the beach earlier. Mostly high-end homes. Beachfront property. Expensive as all get out. In addition to the full-timers, there are vacation rentals, airbnbs, and a few small resort hotels. Our people covered that area pretty thoroughly. Spoke to most of the residents."

On the map Parker saw there were condos beyond the hotels. Too many people. Too many variables.

"And what did your people learn from their interviews?"

"Most residents stated they had no idea about the boat that washed up on the beach and hadn't even noticed it. Some had seen it and wondered what had happened, but had no other information."

Parker studied the map again. There was a house at the west end of the street just before the pavement turned to sand. It was larger than its neighbors. High end, as Kessling had said. The first and most obvious place someone looking for aid might have gone. Perhaps Santana hadn't needed anyone to pick him up.

Parker tapped the paper. "Did you speak to this resident?"

"Let me check." Kessling consulted the folder with the interviews. "No one was home at the time Officer Toulme canvassed the area."

Parker's jaw tensed. "Could that resident be missing? Or worse?" It would be nothing for Santana to take a hostage or kill a homeowner who didn't cooperate.

Graham shook his head. "That was what we feared at first, but my people confirmed the resident was in New York on business. He's been away for over a month."

Before Santana was here. "Do you have the owner's name?"

Kessling pulled out another piece of paper from the folder and read. "John Smith."

Parker scowled. "The two most common first and last names in the US. And Mr. Smith doesn't rent out his property here while he's away?"

"No. Officer Toulme spoke to Smith on the phone. He's in and out and needs to be here on business about five months out of the year. He never knows exactly when, so he doesn't rent out the house."

Something didn't set well about that story. "I don't suppose you could get a search warrant for that house."

"Not enough evidence. And Toulme hasn't been able to get hold of John Smith again to get permission to enter the premises."

Parker let it go for now. "What else do you have?"

Kessling reached for another folder. This one held photos of the inside of Santana's boat.

His blood pressure rising, Parker studied them.

Blood on the helm, the bulkhead, the deck. An empty first aid kit in the cabin. Santana had to patch himself up after the bloody fight he and Parker had had. If only that fight had been enough to end him.

There was little else in the file.

"And finally there was this." Kessling donned a pair of plastic gloves, rose, reached inside the evidence box, and pulled out a rectangular object wrapped in protective plastic.

He set it down in front of Parker and handed him a pair of gloves.

His curiosity roused, Parker slipped on the gloves and peeled away the plastic. Inside was a case of dark red leather.

He set it down and ran his hands over it. Even through the gloves, he could tell it was high-end material. "A gun case."

"Open it." Graham's voice was ominous.

Parker flipped the clasp, lifted the lid, and found a black velvet lining. Just as he feared, the case was empty.

A pamphlet was tucked into a pocket in the lid. He didn't need to read it. "This is for a Mauser parabellum IWA, also known as a Luger. A nine millimeter. Probably from the eighties. An antique. A rare one."

Kessling gestured toward the case. "There's a picture of the weapon in the pamphlet. It's nickel-plated and has art nouveau engraving. Fancy. Says it came with two magazines. Both missing, as is the weapon."

"Why would Santana be carrying an antique?" Graham said.

Parker could think of only one explanation. "Other than the boat itself, Santana didn't prepare. He hadn't stocked it. He didn't expect his plan to fail." It wouldn't have, if it hadn't been for Miranda.

"There's something else behind the pamphlet."

Parker removed the papers from the pocket, and when he did, his back went stiff.

A small brass plate was carved with the words, "To my son."

Son? Parker's mind reeled with the memory of his father's confession last winter in a New York hotel. He'd had an affair with a woman in Boston before Parker had been born.

Watching his reaction, Kessling reached for a water bottle with his gloved hand. "Who do you think gave Santana that gun, Mr. Parker?"

Once more, Parker's gut twisted inside him with disgust and rage. That gift wasn't from Wade Russell Parker Junior. Parker's father hadn't even known he had another son until a few months ago.

At least that was what his father told him.

Parker believed him. What did that inscription mean then? Did Santana have someone as a father figure? Was that where he had gone? There was nothing else here to tell him.

"I have no idea." Parker closed the lid and put the case back in the plastic. "We know one thing for certain, gentlemen. Santana is armed."

As Kessling put the case back in the box, there was a knock on the open door.

"Excuse me, Lieutenant."

Parker gazed past the evidence spread on the table to a woman in a police uniform standing in the doorway. She appeared to be in her late thirties, had a sinewy build, a tall frame, and wore her hair in a short ash blond cut. She reminded him of what Gen might have looked like if she had gone into law enforcement. A career path Parker had never imagined for his daughter.

Like Gen, the expression on the face of the officer in the doorway was deadly serious.

Kessling scowled at the woman. "What is it, Broom?"

Officer Broom's expression remained unchanged. "We've got a tip on that multiple GTA case. The car theft ring we've been tracking."

Kessling sat up straight. "What kind of a tip?"

"CI says they're going to strike again tonight."

"Same place?"

She nodded. "Seaside Motors."

"That dealership has been hit three times in the last month," Kessling explained to Parker.

Parker's brow rose. "In the last month?"

"Correct." Kessling drew in a stiff breath through his nose. "We get a lot of property theft cases around here due to the tourists, but our motor vehicle theft rate is below the national average. This—this is different."

"The reports the owner filed state that only luxury vehicles were taken," Broom explained. "We believe the crew is taking them to the Port of Mobile to be loaded on a ship and sold overseas."

Graham sat up stiffly. "I know of that operation. Coast Guard officers have been keeping an eye on vessels in the docks in Mobile, but haven't found any substantial evidence of theft as yet."

"They transport only a few cars at a time, sir."

"Surveillance cameras?"

"They haven't been operational."

Parker's interest was piqued. "Officer Broom, did you say all the thefts hit the same dealership?"

"Yessir," Broom nodded without hesitation. She'd been told who Parker was. "Seaside Motors."

"And these thefts started shortly after Santana's boat arrived here?"

"They started about a month ago." Evidently Broom wasn't involved in the hunt for Santana and didn't know the details.

"That fits."

Broom turned her attention back to Kessling. "I believe we've got an opportunity to nab this ring if we set up a stakeout tonight, sir. I'd like to get the unit together in the planning room right now."

"I think that's an excellent idea," Parker answered for the sergeant.

All eyes turned to him.

Graham was the first to regain his voice. "What are you saying, Mr. Parker? That there's a connection between Santana and this car theft ring?"

Parker's brain was racing. "We all know Santana had criminal operations all over the country."

"And you think this ring is one of them?"

"Or he started it with people he had in the area already. If he was short of cash, it would be a way to get some quickly." And only the good Lord knew what he was going to do with it.

Graham nodded thoughtfully. "It's a possibility. There has to be some reason Santana chose this spot to run his boat aground. I'd say it's worth looking into."

"It would prove more fruitful than going door-to-door." Parker patted the stack of folders on the table. "And in order to facilitate the operation, I'd like to join you on that stakeout tonight."

Graham looked at Kessling. "That's up to you."

"If you feel that strongly, Mr. Parker, I'll approve it. That good with you?" he said to Broom. "It's your operation."

"Yessir. We can always use all the manpower we can muster."

Parker got to his feet. "Let's head to your planning room then."

With a nod Kessling rose, and the three men exited the room.

As he followed the others down the same hallway, Parker's spirits began to rise. If his guess was right, if Santana was working with this theft ring, he could get a solid lead on the monster's whereabouts tonight. And if he was here in Gulf Shores, they might have him in custody before morning.

In the meantime the only problem was, again—what to tell Miranda.

CHAPTER FIFTEEN

Miranda sat in the cafeteria of Suburban General Hospital, spooning the last bit of beef stew into her mouth. The grub wasn't half bad, contrary to what the two young interns had said. Especially with the bottle of Tabasco sauce she'd doused it with.

Still not spicy enough for her, but she was surprised a hospital would even have Tabasco, since there might be ulcer patients around. Anyway, she had decided to be grateful for the little things.

The big things were a different story.

She ran her hand over the see-through cover of the report CEO Bryant Williamson had given her.

"Inquiry into the Hilda Steele Case." Same title she'd seen on Ms. Jaworski's computer screen.

Miranda had waited to eat before reading it, but now she was rethinking that decision. Just the cover had the beef stew turning to a hard lump in her stomach.

"Get it over with," she grumbled at herself.

She wiped her mouth, pushed away her bowl, and forced herself to open the thing.

Okay. Not so bad.

The first part was a summary of her mother's work history with Suburban General.

As Miranda already knew, her mother had started out on the cleaning staff. But she had to stop and stare at the date of hire.

It was two months after her father had left. Miranda had just turned six.

She didn't recall much about that time, except for a burning ache in her heart every day. Her mother had kept to herself. Miranda recalled gazing at her closed bedroom door, longing for a hug from her mother, or to cry with her, or to hear her tell her what Miranda had done to make her father go away. Anything.

But that wasn't Hilda Steele's style.

Instead, Miranda was left feeling completely alone. When her mother did emerge from her room, she'd only rummage around in the kitchen for a meal for the two of them, muttering something about money that Miranda hadn't understood at the time.

Now she realized her mother had been looking for a job to keep a roof over their heads.

Her father had sent money from time to time, but it was sporadic. As Miranda now knew, he had been living a nomad's life, bee-bopping from town to town until he eventually made it to Maui and remarried.

The place where Miranda and Parker had spent their honeymoon. And where she'd reconnected with her father and learned she had a half-brother who'd been murdered.

What her father had done was supposed to be in the past and forgiven, but as she stared at the page of the report, the old resentment started to resurface. He was the free-spirited type who would never get along with someone as serious and no-nonsense as her mother. She'd often wondered what they'd seen in each other.

She wished her mother had talked to her then. They might have gotten close. But she hadn't.

Miranda read on.

After spending seven years on the cleaning crew, Hilda Steele started taking classes part time. She got her CNA certificate, then her LPN diploma.

Miranda had to look up the acronyms. CNA was a certified nursing assistant. It had taken her mother six months instead of the typical three to go through the courses and pass the exam, due to her work schedule.

Again Miranda studied the dates.

Suddenly she recalled the park she'd driven past that morning. Her mother must have just started going to school the night Miranda had gone there with her friends. The night her mother had come looking for her. She must have been tired and frustrated and worried. No wonder she'd been so mad.

Miranda felt a tinge of guilt for putting her through that.

LPN stood for licensed practical nurse. Her mother had worked at that level for several years, and her duties included bathing patients, dressing them, changing dressings, and administering medications. She continued going to school part time while working, had nearly completed her bachelor's degree, and was about to become an RN when the "incident" occurred.

Miranda sat back, taking in the new information.

She felt empty. She'd known her mother had become a nurse, but she didn't know the details. She'd had no idea her mother was so ambitious or how hard she had worked to achieve her goals. No wonder she was never home. If only her mother had talked to her about what she was trying to do. Would Miranda have understood? Maybe she was too young.

Too late now.

She turned the page and sucked in her breath at the subtitle.

"Summary of the Incident."

Miranda zoomed through the few short paragraphs.

"On the night in question, at approximately two a.m. Hilda Steele's body was found on the landing between floors two and three of the Neurosurgery unit." Where Miranda had been earlier. She'd been right about that stairwell.

"Resuscitation was attempted. There was no response. The tray of medications Nurse Steele had been delivering was scattered on the concrete. A sponge was found on the stairs. It was dry, but was assumed to have been wet when it was left there.

"The physician on duty, Dr. Bogart E. Musgrove, was called in. Dr. Musgrove officially pronounced Nurse Steele dead. An autopsy was ordered and the cause of death was found to be a combination of subdural hematoma, heart failure, and fracture of the cervical vertebrae."

Exactly what had been on her mother's death certificate. And that was the doctor who signed that document. Dr. Bogart E. Musgrove. He must have been present at the autopsy, too.

The preliminary conclusion was that a member of the cleaning staff had accidentally dropped the sponge, and Nurse Steele had slipped on it and fallen down the stairs.

Just like Mrs. G had told her.

Miranda read the last sentence of the summary. "Nurse Steele's sudden demise was a shock to our community here at Suburban General, and a great loss to the hospital. She will be sorely missed."

Miranda let out a breath. Wow. She recalled there had been a lot of hospital folk at her mother's funeral, but she didn't realize how respected her mother had been.

She turned the page.

The next section contained a series of interviews with everyone who might have known what had happened that night. Medical personnel Nurse Steele had worked with, anyone who had been on duty in the department, the cleaning staff.

One of the longest interviews was with an RN who often worked with Nurse Steele and who had attended classes with her. Her name was Alice Whitaker.

"If you include Hilda's time on the cleaning crew, I worked with her for sixteen years," Nurse Whitaker told the examiner. "She was on the cleaning crew when I met her. We were talking about our kids one night, and we clicked and became friends. Hilda told me she wanted a better career, and I encouraged her to work toward her nursing degree. She was afraid she wouldn't make it because she hadn't been to school for so long, but I told her she had the drive to do it. And she did."

Wow. Miranda hadn't known her mother had had any friends. Or that she'd discussed her with them. Miranda could just imagine what her mother had told this woman.

"Hilda was one of the hardest working people I know," Nurse Whitaker continued. "She took classes in her spare time and often pulled double shifts. I know she worked two shifts that night. She must have been exhausted, or she would have seen that sponge. She didn't miss things like that. She was sharp."

Her mother certainly never missed anything she had tried to get away with. But Miranda had never thought about how that trait would play out in her mother's professional life.

"I'm really going to miss her."

Miranda read through the rest of the interviews. Most of them said things similar to what Nurse Whitaker had.

But the last interview had Miranda sitting up straight in the hard cafeteria chair.

It was the questioning of Hardwick Yontz, the cleaning person on duty that night. He had been at the hospital for twenty years and said he had worked with Nurse Steele when she first started on the cleaning crew. He knew her well, considered her a friend, and was broken up by what had happened to her. He couldn't believe it.

And then the investigator got tougher than he had with the others. "Did you drop that sponge on the stairs, Mr. Yontz?"

Yontz was their primary suspect.

"No, sir. I did not."

"But you cleaned the staircase that night, correct?"

"Mopped and dried. Like I do every night."

"And you didn't drop the sponge?"

"I did not."

"Are you sure?"

"I'm positive."

"But you spoke to Nurse Steele that night, correct?"

"I worked a double that night, too. I saw Hilda around midnight. She was at the dispensing machine pulling meds. 'Working a double again, Hildy?' I said. 'Yep,' she said. 'Just like you.' We chatted a bit, then went back to work. It was the last time I saw her alive."

"Was that before or after you put the sponge on the stair?"

"I told you I didn't put it there. In fact, I—"

"Thank you for your time."

Again Miranda stared at the page. Why did the examiner cut him off like that? He had more to say. When she got to the "Findings" section on the last page, she realized why.

"After thorough investigation and painstaking efforts, the board has concluded Mr. Hardwick Yontz inadvertently dropped a wet sponge on the west side staircase of the Neurosurgery unit. Before he realized said sponge was missing, Nurse Steele had stepped on the sponge during her nightly rounds and fallen down the stairs, twisting her neck and hitting her head in the process. She also suffered a mild heart attack from the trauma and died instantly. Mr. Yontz was dismissed with a stern reprimand. He received no severance. Again, the

Suburban General family mourns the loss of a valuable employee in Nurse Steele."

Miranda let out a long slow breath and thought about Aunt Lu.

She could give her aunt a copy of this report, but she had a feeling it wouldn't satisfy her.

It didn't satisfy Miranda, either. "Thorough investigation"? Hardly. Sounded more like a hatchet job to her. There was no double checking of the facts, and they wouldn't let the cleaning man defend himself. Maybe it had gone down the way the board concluded, maybe not.

They certainly hadn't proven anything.

She thought of her Aunt's words. "Don't you think she made a few enemies at her job?" Aunt Lu was convinced someone put that sponge on the stairs on purpose.

Was it true? Did Hardwick Yontz do that? He was the most likely suspect. Had he been jealous of her mother after she left the cleaning crew? But maybe one of these other nurses had had it in for her mother. Again, there weren't enough facts.

In frustration, Miranda tapped her fingers on the table. If only she could talk to some of these interviewees and do her own cross-examination.

Her cell buzzed. She dug it out of her pocket and found a text from Parker.

I'm so sorry, darling. This case is lingering on. I hope to book a room for a few hours of sleep and get a flight home in the morning.

Miranda ground her teeth. Parker was shutting her out the same way her mother had. "Lingering on." What did that mean? Had he found Santana? He'd better not put himself in danger.

Before Miranda could decide how to answer, the sound of loud clapping echoing from the corner of the cafeteria caught her attention.

She looked over in that direction and saw a group of hospital workers in variously-colored scrubs gathered around two tables that had been pushed together. The tables were covered with gifts and a half-eaten sheet cake.

A party. Miranda had been so engrossed in reading her report, she hadn't even noticed them when they came in.

At the far end of the table stood a woman opening gifts. Looked like she was on the last of a big pile of them. Helium balloons floated on strings tied to the chair behind her. One of them read, "We'll miss you, Alice."

Must be a retirement party.

Wait. Alice? Miranda grabbed her report and paged through the interviews.

There it was. Alice Whitaker. The nurse who'd worked with her mother for sixteen years. Her mother's friend.

Was that her? She was the right age.

Getting up from the table and tucking the report under her arm, Miranda decided to find out.

CHAPTER SIXTEEN

Miranda got rid of her bowl and tray on a conveyor belt and slowly made her way over to the party. For a moment she watched the woman who was the center of attention.

She had on pale pink scrubs, wore her reddish hair in a neat shoulder-length style, and had the obligatory stethoscope around her neck. She was attractive, but looked her age. Probably from so many years at a stressful job. Still her face had a kind, motherly air to it. A sort of angelic look that reminded her a little of Coco.

Alice held up one of the last gifts. A bright blue T shirt that read, "Retired Nurse. Really."

Once again everyone laughed and applauded.

She swiped a finger under her nose. "Thank you so much, everyone. This means a lot to me. More than I can say. I'll never forget you or my time here. But right now it's time I got you all back to work, or they might fire me."

Everyone laughed again, and chairs squeaked across the floor as the group rose and started to clean up the party remnants. A stocky woman in light blue scrubs moved over to Alice and gave her a hug. "We sure are going to miss you, Alice. You're the best supervisor ever."

"Thank you, Elizabeth. But I think Jessica will do a fine job in my place. Just remember what I've always told you."

"The patient always comes first," said a smiling young man in black scrubs.

"That's right."

The young man leaned over the table to reach for the gifts. "Let me help you carry some of these things."

"That would be nice, Tony. Just take them to my office. I have to start my last shift. And so do all of you."

While the others made their way out, chatting and laughing, Alice lingered at the table, gathering her balloons.

Just the opportunity she needed.

When the last guest had gone through the door, Miranda sidled up to the table. The name tag the woman was wearing gave away her identity, but Miranda decided to be polite. "Excuse me. You wouldn't be Alice Whitaker, would you?"

The nurse looked up in surprise, and then gave her a warm smile. "Yes, that's me. Do I know you?"

Bingo. Miranda resisted the urge to do a fist pump.

Might as well get straight to the point. "I think you knew my mother."

Alice tilted her head and frowned at her. "Your mother?"

Miranda held the report up so Alice could see the cover. "Hilda Steele. You said in your interview you were friends with her."

Alice's smile disappeared as her hand went to her throat, and she sucked in a raspy breath as if she were having a cardiac arrest. Staring at her as if she were a ghost, it took a moment before she could speak. "You—you're Miranda?"

Miranda was surprised the woman remembered her name. "That's right. I'm looking into what happened to my mother. What can you tell me?"

Alice blinked and looked around the room. "Let's go to my office."

"Sure."

CHAPTER SEVENTEEN

Alice grabbed her balloons and led Miranda out of the cafeteria to an elevator bank where they took a car to the third floor.

The balloons bobbing in the air, they moved through a wide bright corridor lined with chair rails, rolling carts, and doors leading into patient's rooms Miranda didn't want to look inside.

Alice stopped for a moment at a light-colored counter where three of the scrub-clad party goers Miranda had seen in the cafeteria were standing.

Alice addressed a tall dark-haired woman in navy scrubs. "Jessica, can you take over for me for a few minutes before we have our daily huddle?"

"Yes, of course." Jessica eyed Miranda with curiosity, but didn't comment.

"Thank you. Let me know if we get an admission."

"Will do."

With a smile that seemed forced, Alice turned and led Miranda down a narrower hall to a small office with a corner desk.

"Have a seat," she said, gesturing to the only guest chair tucked between the desk and the wall.

While the woman fiddled with her balloons, stuffing them into the corner of the ceiling as best she could, Miranda squeezed herself into the seat.

The desk was cluttered with the gifts from the party, which her staff had placed atop neat piles of paperwork, and the room smelled a little like antiseptic.

Ignoring all the presents, Alice reached around to close the door, sat down, and stared at Miranda with the same look she'd had downstairs.

After a moment she shook herself. "I apologize for my reaction, Miranda, but this is quite a shock."

"Is it?"

"Why, yes. I grieved for my friend a long time after she passed. I still think of her often. I still miss her. But I never thought I'd see you again."

"Again?"

"We spoke at the funeral. I don't suppose you remember."

All Miranda remembered about her mother's funeral was a blurry sea of faces and an empty feeling of despair. But that wasn't what she had come here to talk about.

She held up the report again. "I just finished reading this. It seems a little shy on facts, in my opinion."

Alice blinked, still surprised at the sight of the document. "Where did you get that?"

"From your CEO."

"Mr. Williamson gave it to you?"

"Yes, he did."

She blinked, taking that in. "Well, I suppose you're entitled to see it."

"I'm also a private investigator, Ms. Whitaker." Miranda dug out a card and handed it to the woman. "I work for the Parker Investigative Agency in Atlanta."

"You do?"

Her schedule probably kept her too busy to watch TV, or she'd know that from the news, like most other folks around here.

Alice gave her a cautious look. "And are you...still married?"

Her mother really had discussed a lot of her personal life with this woman. It made her uncomfortable, but Miranda refused to show it.

"Remarried," she said curtly. "To the boss."

Her face relaxing into a smile, Alice studied the card with a motherly expression. "Hilda would have been so proud. And please call me Alice."

The last thing Miranda wanted was to get all touchy-feely with her mother's old work friend who already knew too much about her. All she wanted was a little information. "What else can you tell me about the night my mother died...Alice? Other than what's in this report."

Alice smiled sadly. "My, you're direct. Just like Hilda was."

Miranda didn't know how to respond to that. She was getting more uncomfortable by the minute, but she needed answers. "Why don't you just tell me what you remember."

Alice drew in a breath and brushed off the lap of her scrubs. "Well, then. Let me think."

"Were you on duty that night?"

Alice sat back and thought a moment. "Yes I was. I was on third shift and came on duty just before midnight. It was a busy night. Your mother had worked second shift and was getting ready to put in another eight hours. She looked tired. I told her to go home, but she refused."

"You didn't argue with her? You didn't insist she go home?"

"I had been her mentor when she started, but I wasn't her boss at the time. Besides, once Hilda made up her mind, there was no changing it. And she often pulled doubles."

So Alice had said in her interview, and Miranda had never been able to change her mother's mind about anything, either. "Did you work alongside my mother that night?"

"No. We had separate assignments. I remember seeing her filling her tray with meds in the supply room. We had metal trays back then. That was the old way. So inefficient and error-prone. We haven't used them in years. We use carts now."

"So you saw her take the tray of meds down the stairs?"

"I saw her leave the supply room. I knew she had patients on two floors."

"Why did she take the stairs instead of the elevator?"

"The Neuro unit was divided between two floors then. Prep and ICU were on the third floor, Recovery and Critical Care on the second. It was a less than ideal configuration, but back then, we were so short of funds, nothing could be done about it. After Mr. Williamson came on board, things got better. We got new equipment, more staff, and construction began on this wing. Now everything's on one floor the way it should be. But when Hilda worked here, we were always short-staffed, and the elevators were slow. Your mother didn't like to wait. She often took the stairs."

"You knew that?"

"Yes."

"Did anyone else know that?"

"I suppose so. A lot of personnel took the stairs to save time."

And all the coworkers who knew her mother's habit made for a lot of potential suspects. But Miranda didn't think this woman was one of them. "What do you think happened?"

Alice's voice took on a sad tone. "Well, the day after, Administration sent out a memo saying your mother had had an unfortunate accident, and they were asking each department to tighten safety measures. They also said the board was conducting an investigation into the incident. They were trying to suppress rumors, or worse yet, loss of personnel."

"And did you buy that?"

Alice's brow rose. "Are you asking if I think it was an accident?"

"That's right."

"What else would it be?"

Miranda gave the woman a patient smile. "I don't think my mother would have gotten along with everyone she worked with. Surely she made some enemies."

Alice frowned for a moment, then sighed. "You're right. Hilda could be gruff. We worked on that. Over the years her people skills improved a great deal."

Miranda had never seen that. A little hard to believe, but she hadn't had many conversations with her mother after she'd left home and married Leon.

She tapped the report. "What about this Hardwick Yontz?"

"I'm sorry. I wasn't given a copy of that report."

"You mean you don't know what the board's findings were?"

"I know a few weeks after it happened Hardwick was dismissed. The rumors were that the board felt he was responsible."

"And what did you think?"

"I didn't have an opinion."

"No opinion about how your good friend died?"

Alice drew in a breath. "Miranda, here in the Neuro unit, many of our patients are stroke victims, cancer victims. Some are here for spinal surgery, but several suffer from aneurysms, brain tumors, hemorrhages. As you might imagine, in this line of work we deal with tragedy on a regular basis. I find it's best not to dwell on what we have no control over. I accepted what happened to Hilda and moved on, just as I do when we lose a patient. We don't always have the luxury of an explanation."

Miranda didn't know what to say to that.

She'd had no idea her mother had worked with people who were dying. It made her feel an odd sort of connection with her. A feeling she couldn't quite process. She worked with dead people, too.

But that was different.

Miranda had to respect Alice's feelings and the work she did, but things still didn't add up. And in her line of work, you didn't leave loose ends hanging.

Trying to sound gentler, she pressed on. "This report says that Hardwick Yontz, the cleaning person, accidentally dropped a sponge on the stairs, and my mother slipped on it."

Alice's brows rose. She hadn't heard the board's conclusion. Or she'd dismissed it. But now she raised her palms. "Then that's probably what happened."

"Did you know Hardwick Yontz?"

"Yes, everyone did. He was with us for years. He was always pleasant. He and Hilda were friends."

So he'd said in his interview. "Was he on duty that night?"

Her brow creased. "Yes, he was. I believe he was working a double shift, too. I remember he and Hilda were talking before she went into the supply room to get her meds. In fact…"

"What?"

"It seemed as if they were arguing. Bickering, really."

"Over what?"

"I'm not sure. It was probably nothing."

Or it was everything. Her mother might have made enemies Alice Whitaker wasn't aware of or didn't want to admit to. "Do you know what happened to Hardwick Yontz? I mean, where he went after he was dismissed?"

"No, I'm afraid not. I'm sorry I can't be of more help." She paused a moment, then reached across the desk for Miranda's arm. "I'm so sorry she's gone. She loved you very much."

Miranda couldn't help scoffing at that. "Did she?"

"Of course. I know, she didn't always show it."

Miranda let out a cough. "How do you know that?"

"We talked about our children a lot. I was raising two boys at the time you were little. Hilda confessed to me once that she hadn't been a very good mother. She'd been devastated when your father left, and realized she didn't know how to raise a child. Your father had always taken care of you. All she knew was to teach you how harsh life could be, and that there was no time for fun and games, as she put it."

"She did do that."

"When you got married so young, Hilda knew you were trying to get away from her."

She did? Miranda stared at Alice. This nurse knew things about her she didn't know herself.

Alice peered back at her with a piercing gaze. "I think I need to tell you something."

Miranda's stomach turned sour. "What?"

Alice let go of Miranda's arm. Taking a moment, she drew in a breath. Then she said it. "Somehow Hilda found out your husband...wasn't treating you very well."

Miranda was stunned. "How?"

"I think she had a friend who knew one of your neighbors."

Another friend Miranda had never heard of.

"The neighbor had heard a lot of yelling and banging coming from your house. And screaming."

That had been her, all right.

"There was an ambulance at your house, too."

Miranda shivered at the words. She remembered that night. She'd been afraid Leon was going to kill her and had gotten up the nerve to call 911.

Leon had been furious, but he'd backed off for a while. The cops came that night, too. But Leon was a cop, too. And so well connected, she knew it wouldn't do any good to press charges.

Miranda looked into Alice's warm blue eyes. They were filled with compassion. "Hilda told me something after she heard what the neighbor said."

"What?"

"One night, she went to your house and found your husband."

Miranda's chin dropped. "She did?" She must have been out shopping or something.

"She told him if he ever hurt you again, she'd destroy him."

"Destroy him? How?"

"She said she'd make sure he lost his job and he'd go to jail."

Miranda nearly dropped her report on the floor. "My mother said that to Leon?"

"That's what she told me. As I said, she loved you very much."

No wonder Leon had backed off.

Her mother had loved her? Had stood up for her? That was hard to believe. And then the memories of the night she'd called 911 began to form in her mind.

She recalled standing outside next to the ambulance telling an officer what had happened. She didn't remember what she'd told him, but she knew the weather had been warm. Someone was talking about back-to-school shopping for their kids, so it had to be late summer. Her mother died just before Thanksgiving. The same year.

Suddenly feeling cold and shaky, Miranda looked up at Alice. "When did my mother go to my house to see Leon? I mean, how long before she died?"

Alice put a hand to her head, forcing herself to remember.

When she did, her face turned a little pale. "As best as I can recall, just a few months."

CHAPTER EIGHTEEN

Reeling, Miranda sat on the bed in her fancy hotel suite, the hamburger she'd ordered from room service going cold on the tray.

After leaving the hospital, she'd driven around in circles for hours in a daze, barely aware of where she was going. She'd cruised through her old neighborhood, past the park, past her mother's house, past the house where she'd lived with Leon.

That was where she'd come to a stop in the middle of the street and peered hard at the modest house the new owners had painted yellow with its pretty yard, trying to imagine her mother at the door telling Leon to leave her alone.

How could that be true? Her mother sticking up for her? Impossible. But Alice Whitaker wasn't the type to lie, and her mother wouldn't have thought to make up a story like that.

Miranda got up from the hotel chair and went to the window, hugging herself as she stared out at the dark street below.

Her mother had loved her, Alice had said. She would have been proud of her for becoming a private investigator.

Talk about a seismic shift.

All these years, Miranda had never believed her mother had loved her. She had been nothing but a burden to her. "Life is hard," she'd tell her when she was angry with her. "There's no place for fun and games."

Miranda had thought her mother hated her for just being a kid. Had she really been protecting her from making the same mistake she had? For marrying someone who'd leave?

And then Miranda had gone and married Leon.

Leon.

He must have been enraged when her mother told him to leave her alone. He would have wanted to get her back for that.

Was *he* the one who put that sponge on the stairs?

She spun around and went to the laptop she'd left running on the table in the corner. She put her fingers on the keyboard, but they didn't move.

How could she prove anything?

Police station records that showed when officers clocked in and out? It was seventeen years ago. They'd probably used cards back then. Even if they were electronic, they'd be archived. No, probably purged by now. And wouldn't be at all conclusive.

Maybe she could find someone Leon worked with back then. But how could another officer remember where Leon was on the night her mother died? And even if he did, why should he tell her?

She could contact Becker. Maybe he could think of something. But Fanuzzi would probably answer the phone. She couldn't handle that right now.

Rubbing her temples, she sat there for several more minutes. Then she got up, shoved the dinner cart with the hamburger into the hall, and took a shower.

When she climbed into bed, she felt numb.

She glanced at her phone and saw Parker's message from that afternoon. She grunted out loud. "Why are you chasing ghosts when you should be here?"

She longed to talk to him. She longed for his warmth, for his arms around her. Raising a finger, she hovered over the phone.

Then she put it down. No, he could be in the middle of something dangerous. That thought made her remember she was still too mad at him for words.

She turned off the light, gave her pillow a few socks, and laid her head down. She was exhausted, emotionally drained. Her head hurt, her stomach ached, she felt sick.

Her mind started to swim with the images she'd seen today. Bryant Williamson's kind face, Alice's warm smile, her old house, all swirling around in her head in a cloudy mist. Instinctively, she reached across the bed and found nothing.

Oh, Parker. She missed him so much.

And as she fell asleep, all she knew was that she had never felt so much alone.

CHAPTER NINETEEN

It was just past midnight.

Parker sat in the passenger seat of Lieutenant Graham Chadwick's unmarked Camry, peering through a pair of borrowed binoculars at the darkened entrance to Seaside Motors.

No gate, he noted. Just a dirt road through a patch of tall weeds—the road they were parked beside, a short distance from the entrance. It led to a wider dirt road, which led to the highway beyond.

In light of the recent thefts, security at Seaside Motors was strangely lacking. Parker had a weakness for luxury cars, and it angered him to think they were being taken so easily.

In the planning meeting, Officer Broom had said the owner of Seaside Motors couldn't explain how the incidents had happened. The vehicles taken were theft-proof. Their keys and fobs were locked in a system controlled by a keypad inside the office. He had already lost several hundred thousand dollars and was very upset. He demanded the police do something.

Again Parker scanned the yard.

The dealership had approximately ninety vehicles sitting in a lot stretching across a flat piece of land a few miles north of the police station. At the moment everything was silent and still. There was only the hum of insects in a nearby field, interrupted occasionally by a passing car on the highway in front of the dealership.

Out of sight, Broom and Kessling were in a squad car parked along a utility road at the rear of the dealership. Additional squad cars were waiting farther away. The surveillance cameras had been repaired and were ready to record.

Broom's voice came over the remote. "Everyone's in position. Subjects should be approaching shortly. Nobody move until I give the order."

"Roger that," Graham replied.

They had to wait until vehicles were actually taken from the lot in order to prove theft.

It was a warm, muggy night, but clear. They didn't want to run the engine, so there was no A/C, and they had the windows down. The borrowed Glock in the borrowed shoulder holster under the suit jacket Parker wore felt heavy.

He checked his phone.

There was still no answer to the text he'd sent that afternoon. He could almost feel the heat of Miranda's rage singeing his fingertips.

After Officer Broom's planning meeting that afternoon, he had checked into a nearby hotel for a few hours sleep, as he'd told her, and had had a good meal before meeting Graham at the police station. He'd expected a reply before now.

Parker looked at the screen again and let out a grunt of frustration.

"Trouble on the homefront?"

With a reluctant grin, Parker looked into Graham's keen gaze. "Still as perceptive as you were at the Agency, I see."

Graham knew Sylvia had passed, and that Parker had remarried. He also knew who Miranda Steele was, but didn't ask why she wasn't here. He had always been discreet.

Graham chuckled. "I'm having the same issue. Rachel was pretty upset when I told her about this stake-out tonight."

"Oh?"

"When I took the job of senior intelligence specialist three years ago, I promised her no more field work. It was a desk job and I was content with that."

Until this matter with Santana came up.

"She's worried. I understand that. We have three little ones to think about." Graham took out his phone and scrolled to a photo.

A lovely brown-haired woman was perched next to Graham on a bench before a photography studio background. A baby boy on her lap sucked his fingers while two girls who were probably seven or eight grinned eagerly at the camera on the floor beneath the parents.

Parker's heart warmed. "What a fine family you have."

"I'm proud of them. Mia loves art, and Zoe is into swimming. She hopes to be in the Olympics one day."

"Ambitious dreams."

"I encourage that. Of course, Noah is too young for anything but toys."

As Parker smiled at the image, he couldn't help thinking about Antonio and the baby that would soon be born to him and Coco. And the child Joan Fanuzzi was carrying as well. Dave Becker was more beside himself about being a father than ever.

Parker longed for that life. Safety, security, home.

Miranda might be angry with him now, but at least she was safe in bed in the penthouse. As soon as he found Santana and dealt with him, he'd put Judd in charge of the Agency, and they could retire in earnest. He'd let Judd decide what to do with the errant Curt Holloway.

Graham put his phone away and grew serious again. "Do you really think Santana is operating this ring?"

Parker had to admit the idea didn't seem as appealing after a long nap and a meal. "There's enough evidence to bear out the idea."

"But on the other hand, he might not be involved at all."

"Another possibility."

"Which means after tonight, we'll be back at square one with our search for him."

Parker didn't want to accept that idea. Or admit it was mostly his gut telling him that Santana was in the area and up to no good. As he searched for other facts to bolster the theory, the roar of an engine rang out in the distance.

Parker raised his binoculars as quickly as Graham.

He watched as an empty double-decker vehicle carrier turned onto the dirt road from the highway. It clattered toward them for a short distance, then turned onto the narrower road and into the dealership's open entrance. Taking its time, the large tractor-trailer circled the lot and finally squealed to a stop in the middle of an aisle of cars.

Two men in dark clothes and ball caps hopped out of the truck's cab and moved toward its rear. While one of them released a safety switch and lowered the ramp to the upper deck, a third man emerged from the back of the showroom. He also wore dark clothes and a ball cap.

Graham sat up with a snort. "Is that a Seaside employee?"

The man in question trotted over to the one at the controls and handed him something. Keys.

"It's an inside job," Parker growled.

The three men spread out over the lot and got into various vehicles.

A Mercedes reached the carrier first. The man inside backed the car up the ramp to the top of the cab, secured it in place, and climbed down the metal ladder at the side of the carrier.

Then he ran to fetch another vehicle while the second car rolled up the ramp.

Before long, six luxury cars had been loaded onto the rig. Two Mercedes, three Lamborghinis, and a Tesla.

The men secured the vehicles, then moved back toward the truck's cab. For a long moment they stood in a circle, smoking and talking, the employee apparently giving further directions.

He was in charge.

He took two envelopes from his jacket, handed one to each man, and the accomplices broke away and trotted over to another car parked a few aisles away.

They drove the truck here, but they were probably taking the employee's vehicle to his residence.

Covering his bases. Use one team to load the cars here, another to unload them at the Port of Mobile, and none of them would be able to testify about the others.

Parker adjusted his binoculars to get a closer look at the employee. Big, bulky, dressed in black leather. Looking anxious, he removed his ball cap to wipe his brow.

Parker's breath stopped.

Bald head with a black spider tattoo.

The employee shouted something to the man who was now unlocking a sedan. Parker couldn't make out the words, but he heard the accent.

Ukrainian.

"That's definitely one of Santana's men."

"How do you know?"

Before Parker could answer, the employee shoved his cigarette in his mouth, climbed into the rig on the driver's side, and started the engine.

The sedan spun around, hit the gas, and sped past the truck, flying out of the entrance.

Broom's voice crackled through the remote. "Suspects leaving the scene. In pursuit. Proceed with caution."

Graham turned the key in the ignition, and the Camry came to life just as the carrier rumbled over the road in front of them. Graham spun onto the dirt and followed it past a tractor parked in the weeds.

The truck made a turn onto the wider path and headed for the highway.

Graham kept his distance until Broom's squad car shot around them, lights flashing.

But instead of pulling over, the carrier truck sped up. It swung onto the highway, running the light, and causing a lone driver to screech to a halt and honk his horn.

Broom turned on the siren.

The Ukrainian ignored it.

Graham turned onto the highway and pulled up behind Broom's car. "Where are the other squad cars?"

"Pursuing the sedan, I hope," Parker said. The vehicle driven by the accomplices was nowhere in sight.

"Broom needs to pull that truck over."

"She's trying not to escalate the situation, I'd say."

"Wouldn't be my approach."

Graham always liked to bring things to a close fast.

Broom's voice echoed through her loud speaker. "Pull over. That's right. You in the car carrier. Pull over."

"Now she's getting tough," Graham chuckled.

Parker wasn't smiling. His gut went tight as the truck barreled through another intersection, nearly hitting another car.

Broom had had enough. Her siren screaming, she pulled into the inside lane and zoomed to the side of the truck.

In the passenger seat, Kessling opened the window and barked through a bullhorn. "Pull over."

The driver sped up again. It was doing well over eighty.

Broom's car surged past the truck and out of sight.

Graham shook his head. "That won't work."

Parker agreed.

With the Camry at the trailer's rear, Parker drew the Glock from his shoulder holster and leaned out the open passenger window. Ignoring the odor of burning diesel fuel, he aimed for the outside tire of the rear axle.

He fired twice. Hit the tread.

The carrier swerved. Straightened. And sped up again.

"Bullet-resistant tires," Graham growled.

"Exactly." Adding proof to the theory Santana's organization was funding this ring.

Before Parker could get back inside the Camry, he caught sight of the hood of Broom's squad car.

She had pulled it crosswise into the next intersection, about twenty yards in front of the oncoming truck to block its progress.

Bad move.

A few seconds later, it happened.

With a loud crunching sound, the truck plowed into the squad car, spinning it all the way around, no doubt totaling it. Parker could feel the crash in his teeth.

A string of curses came over the remote. Broom sounded stunned.

Praying Broom and Kessling weren't hurt, Parker sat back down in disgust.

Sirens filled the air.

In the next lane, two more screaming police cars whizzed by the Camry. One of them attempted to stop the truck again. From the passenger side, an officer brandished a weapon at the driver.

"You're under arrest," said his partner through the loud speaker. "Pull over now."

Again the truck zoomed ahead. Speeding up, the cop cars responded in kind, one behind the other.

An officer in the first car fired.

He hit the door of the cab, doing little damage.

In answer, the truck swerved and thrust both police vehicles to the side of the road like an elephant batting away flies. The cars spun around and crashed into the guardrail with an ear-splitting grind, sending sparks into the night.

Now Parker was furious. "Can you get alongside that carrier?"

Just as angry, Graham nodded. "This Camry might look modest, but it can do a hundred and thirty-five."

"And we'll need every bit of that."

Graham pressed the accelerated and whizzed up to the truck's side. In the flash of passing streetlights, Parker could see the gleam of one of the Lamborghinis in the trailer. He studied the carrier's framework.

"Get me close to that ladder." It would do.

"What are you thinking, Mr. Parker?"

"Do you have a better idea?"

"Not at the moment." Graham steered the Camry as close as he dared to the eighteen-wheeler.

"Keep the car as steady as you can."

Frowning his disapproval, Graham gripped the wheel tightly. "What do you want me to tell your wife if you don't make it?"

"That I was thinking of her."

Parker holstered his gun, leaned out of the window again, and grabbed hold of the metal ladder on the side of the rig with both hands.

"Back away. Now."

As Graham obeyed his command, Parker pulled himself up and onto the ladder.

The truck's wind burst nearly tossed him off and onto the asphalt below, but he managed to keep his footing and hold on.

His hair, his tie and jacket flailing in the gust, Parker steadied himself and began to climb.

One. Two. Three. Four rungs and he was at the top.

The first car had been loaded backwards and sat atop the roof of the cab.

The hood of the silver blue Mercedes gleamed in the whizzing street lamps like a magical lake. Grabbing tightly onto the truck's crossbar, Parker pulled himself up and onto the Mercedes.

The force of the air turbulence nearly knocked him over.

He held onto the bar, his knees bent, like a water skier. Without warning, the driver jerked the truck into the left lane.

Parker lost his balance, let go of the crossbar, and slid across the Mercedes to the railing on the other side.

He clutched the support tie holding the car in place just before going over the side, dangled beside its front tire for several terrifying moments. But he wasn't giving up. His palms burning, he gritted his teeth and pulled himself back on top of the Mercedes.

Just as he regained his balance, another police car came up alongside the truck on the right.

The officer shouted words Parker couldn't hear over the engine and the sirens. But he saw the weapon in his hand.

Before he could fire, the truck's passenger window exploded. Good Lord. The driver had a weapon and wasn't afraid to use it.

The squad car swerved to avoid being shot, slammed into the truck's middle axle, and spun off into the guardrail, tearing the fender with another ear-splitting screech.

Parker had had enough of this joy ride.

Resolve burning inside him, he used the tie to lower himself onto the floor of the trailer's upper deck, and inched toward the front of the truck, just over the cab.

He had to act before the driver made another reckless move.

Praying that the tie would hold, he crouched down next to the Mercedes's rear tire, pushed off like a repelling rock climber, and flung himself feet first through the shattered passenger window.

He felt the crunch of broken glass as his dress shoes hit the seat, and he took in the large bald tattooed man and the smell of cigarettes and body odor.

Then he caught the gleam of the .44 Magnum on the seat next to the driver.

The man reached for the gun, but before he could grab it, Parker put his hand under his coat, drew his police-issued Glock, and shoved the barrel into the man's cheek.

"Stop this truck or your brains will be on the street alongside those police cars."

The man's lips pulled back in a grimace. But he hesitated for only a second, and finally pressed the brake.

CHAPTER TWENTY

An hour later, Parker stood at the two-way mirror to the Gulf Shores police station's interrogation room watching Officer Broom and Sergeant Kessling go after the large tattooed man sitting across from them.

Broom wore a bandage on a cut over her eye, and Kessling was nursing a sore arm from the vehicular assault by the man. Broom's squad car had been totaled.

Parker was grateful their injuries hadn't been worse.

"Where did you think you were taking that truck?" Broom asked for the third time.

The man shrugged. "Where my employer told me to take it."

"Oh? Does he own another dealership in the area?"

"You would have to ask him."

Kessling slapped a fist down on the table. "Your two accomplices are singing like jaybirds in the other interrogation rooms."

The man smiled at Kessling. "I don't think so."

Parker had been told it had taken several officers to catch up to the sedan. And then there had been a long foot chase. Shots were fired, but no one had been injured. Finally the two other drivers had been taken into custody, and were indeed in neighboring rooms being questioned.

He didn't think the pair would be able to tell them much.

Broom tried to compose herself. "If you cooperate with us, the DA might cut you a deal."

Again the man shrugged. "Grand theft auto is only three years."

"Think again," Kessling barked. "In this state, first degree felony grand theft is punishable up to twenty years. Per count."

"I guess I will need to call my lawyer then."

The inevitable outcome.

Looking thoroughly disgusted, Broom and Kessling rose and left the room.

Parker met them in the hall. It was his turn.

Broom extended a hand. "Thank you again for your help tonight, Mr. Parker."

"My pleasure."

Kessling smirked. "I hope you get what you need in there."

"I intend to."

Kessling buzzed the door for him, and Parker stepped into the interrogation room.

The man in the chair turned to him and started.

The precise reaction Parker expected.

Then he narrowed his eyes as he realized Parker wasn't who he'd thought.

Parker strolled over to the table and sat down in the chair Kessling had vacated. "Good evening, Mr. Smith. Or should I say good morning."

It was the wee hours of the night.

The man continued to stare at him.

John Smith. The name on the driver's license the man had been carrying. And the address on the license was none other than the luxury home on the west end of the Gulf Hills residential community.

Where Santana's boat had been found. Just as Parker had suspected, the place was a front. And the man's real name was more likely Vladimir or Dmitri. He had no doubt come from Udar, in Ukraine where so many of Santana's men had been trained.

"I said I want a lawyer."

"You'll get one, but I don't think he'll get you out of this one."

"We'll see about that. I am not talking until I get one." He sat back and folded his meaty arms over a bulky chest.

"I'm not with the police."

"FBI?"

"Private investigator." Parker took out his phone and scrolled to the photo of Santana from the Gulf Shores article. He slid it across the table and let Mr. John Smith take in the image for a while.

He remained silent, no doubt wondering at the similarity between the photo and Parker.

He tapped the screen. "This man is at large and wanted by the FBI. We believe he's in the area."

"I never saw him before."

"Is he running this operation?"

"I don't have to tell you anything." He set his jaw and looked up at the window.

Parker picked up the phone and studied the photo. "No, you don't. But I can't imagine he'll be happy with what happened tonight."

John Smith sniffed.

Parker leaned toward the man. "Not only have you lost several hundred thousand dollars worth of inventory, you've drawn attention to yourself. You're going to be on the news."

The chair creaked as the man shifted his weight. He was growing uncomfortable.

"In addition, I know from personal experience this man is capable of infiltrating prisons and doing away with those he deems no longer necessary. If the FBI had him in custody, he wouldn't be able to do that."

Parker watched his words penetrate the man's brain. He was beginning to realize his options were limited.

Finally the man turned back and rested an arm on the table as if he were in charge of this negotiation. He gestured to the phone. "That man is not in charge any longer. Someone new is."

"How do you know that?"

"We got word there had been a shake-up."

"What do you mean?"

The man glared at Parker as if he were an imbecile. "I mean something went wrong with some operation and now somebody else is in charge."

Beasley, Parker guessed. The senator who had been Santana's accomplice in his scheme to rule the world and destroy half the country. Though Beasley was in prison. Perhaps it was someone else. A secondary Santana had designated in a worse case scenario. Parker wasn't interested in those details.

He waited for the man to speak again. At last, he did.

"He came here about a month ago. Knocked on my door."

"The house in Gulf Hills?"

The Ukrainian nodded.

"He was a mess, but he did not stop to clean up. All he wanted was a car."

"A car?"

"One that would not be easily recognized. The only one we had at Seaside was an old Cutlass Cruiser with over a hundred thousand miles on it. I did not think it would go very far, but he took it anyway."

"Color?"

"Brown. Dirty brown."

"Plates?"

"They would be in the records. We recorded it as a sale. He cut the GPS. I do not think you will find him."

Parker's mind began to race. So Santana was not in the area. He had left by car. Over a month ago. John Smith was right. It would be almost impossible to track him down now.

"I don't suppose he told you where he was going."

"He said the car needed to get him to Kentucky."

Parker was surprised by the admission. "Where in Kentucky?"

"He didn't say."

There had to be more. Just a little more to go on. "He didn't mention anything? A hotel? A road?"

John Smith sat back and shook his head. He rubbed his chin. And then he sat up.

"Wait. He did name a town. It had a funny name. Beans? Berkeley? No. Bardstown. That was it. He said he only had to get as far as Bardstown, Kentucky."

CHAPTER TWENTY-ONE

Parker left the police station and headed back to his hotel room.

He longed for sleep. Instead he used his phone to find the most direct route to Bardstown Kentucky. Over nine hours by car.

Too long.

He packed his things, checked out, and headed to the airport. Lucky enough to find a three-fifty am flight, he took it to Nashville, rented his third vehicle in two days, and headed for I-65. It was the flattest, most direct route to Bardstown, though it was a typical interstate, with nothing but multiple lanes of mile after mile of winding asphalt.

Parker forced himself to stay awake and scrutinize the roadsides.

"John Smith's" words played over and over in his mind. "An old Cutlass Cruiser with over a hundred thousand miles on it. I did not think it would go very far, but he took it anyway."

Could it be that Santana's old Cutlass Cruiser had broken down along the way?

Guesswork. It was all guesswork. Hunches, suppositions, hypotheses based on nothing but the word of a career criminal.

But it was the only thing he had.

Before Parker left Gulf Shores, Graham had assured him Kentucky authorities would be checking the logs of all five major airports in the state. The FBI would join that venture, and police in local towns would be on alert for Santana. His picture would be in the area news programs soon.

Was it all too late?

Where could that monster have been going in Kentucky? Not the area Parker would have guessed he would go. Santana lived a rich man's life. He liked luxury and city culture. Boston. Not rural pastures and horse farms.

Once again, the dark dreams and memories that had haunted Parker since his capture tugged at the corners of his mind. The fear, the terror, the utter despair. He had shared them with no one. Not even Miranda.

Miranda.

He was doing this for her. For both of them. But she would never understand that, would she? Still, if he could find Santana tonight and put him away, she would come to see he was right to take this risk.

Two hours later, he reached Elizabethtown and turned onto the west end of the Bluegrass Parkway. It was an area of farms and forests and little towns of no more than ten-thousand people.

The road curved monotonously around low hills, making Parker's head nod. He was fifteen miles outside of Bardstown. There was nothing here.

His hunch had been wrong, if he could even call it a hunch.

There would be a long search in the area. It would take months. And it all might be for nothing. A month ago, Santana might have left this place unnoticed. For all Parker knew, he lied to his henchman and drove the car somewhere else.

He could be anywhere.

But then Parker spotted something. Or thought he had. The sun was just beginning to come up through the trees ahead when he saw it again.

Far ahead in the very end of his headlight beam, he saw the glint of metal. A fender? Or a hallucination. Or a dream, if he had fallen asleep at the wheel.

Shaking himself, he peered through the windshield. He hadn't been dreaming.

He began to brake. There were no other drivers nearby. He slowed the car to a crawl and rolled onto the grass of a nearby hill alongside the road.

He turned on his brights and got out of the rental, ignoring the chill in the early morning air. His jaw set, he focused on the gleam he had seen and made his way downhill through several yards of ankle-high weeds that soaked his pant legs with hoarfrost. And then he stopped.

There it was.

Under a clump of trees, just over the hill's crest sat an old dirty brown Cutlass Cruiser.

CHAPTER TWENTY-TWO

Slowly she strolled over the warm white sand. The sky was a brilliant blue. The air was fresh and clean, and the wind blew her hair over her face.

Frothy white waves washed over her toes, making her giggle as she danced away from the water, the hem of her loose gauzy gown flowing around her bare legs.

It was peaceful here. Fun.

"No. No fun. No games." The sudden voice behind her reverberated like thunder, shaking the ground.

Her heart hammering, she spun around and glared at the huge craggy mountain looming before her. The sky went dark and stormy. Lightning split through the clouds as the mountain spewed fire from its peak. Rocks tumbled down its side and bounced on the sand, coming straight for her, as if the mountain was hurling them at her.

One of them caught her arm and tore the flesh open.

She screamed. "Stop, Mama. You're hurting me."

"When are you going to learn? Life is no picnic."

The bellowing mountain began moving toward her.

Fear blinded her. She turned and stumbled away as fast as she could.

But she could hear the mountain breathing behind her. It began to roar. More rocks smacked against her legs, and she fell.

Her eyes filled with tears. "Stop it."

She had to get away, but the sand beneath her was growing rocky, too.

She did her best to crawl over the wet shale, but she got nowhere.

Another boulder whirled past her and splashed into the ocean.

Again she screamed.

The waves were far away now. Her face was wet with tears, matting her hair. She pulled her hair out of her eyes, and another booming roar sounded, shaking the earth.

But this time it came from another mountain that was rising up before her.

"When will you learn you can never escape me?"

That was another voice. A familiar voice.

Another huge rock came hurling from the second mountain. It tumbled down a cliff and rolled straight at her.

Finally getting her bearings, she rose and stepped out of its way just in time.

Gasping with fear, she looked up.

With a great creaking noise, a large figure pulled out of the mountainside.

It was a man.

He glared down at her, fury in his eyes. "You'll never get away from me, you stupid whore. I am always here. You must be punished."

Growing smaller, he lurched toward her, grabbed her arm and twisted.

Pain shot through her, but she managed to keep her footing.

She bent her arm and swung around, using the weight of her body to free herself from his grip.

Then she spied one of the boulders at her feet. She picked it up in both hands, held it over her head as she took aim, and hurled it at him with all her might.

The pillow flew across the room, hit the wall with a soft thud, and fell to the carpeted floor.

With a jolt, Miranda opened her eyes and sucked in a breath. Her heart was still pounding.

She looked around. Hotel suite. Chicago. Right.

And she was on the floor next to the bed.

Catching her breath, she stared at the pillow she'd thought was a rock lying innocently next to the dresser.

Nightmare. Again.

Light came from a nearby window. It was morning.

Rise and shine.

Starting to get up, she found her upper arm was sore. She must have wrenched it when she fell out of bed.

Good grief.

When were the bad dreams going to end? If Parker had been here, he would have caught her. No, she wasn't going to indulge those thoughts. She was still mad at him.

Getting to her feet, she brushed herself off, went to the nightstand, and checked her phone.

Nothing.

Huh.

Instead of worrying about Parker, she went to the closet and put on the spare suit she'd packed. It was a nice deep gray herringbone, with a matching lightweight knit top to go under the jacket.

A pair of matching pumps completed the outfit.

She didn't know who she'd be trying to impress today, but she was ready. Her agenda today would be research.

After packing up her laptop, she got her key and headed down to the hotel restaurant.

She was starving.

CHAPTER TWENTY-THREE

Two pancakes, three scrambled eggs and four cups of hot black coffee later, Miranda hadn't gotten any farther than she had last night.

By some miracle, she'd managed to hack into the local police department's employee files, but she couldn't get the work hours of the current offices let alone those who had worked there seventeen years ago.

She wasn't going to prove Leon was at Suburban General the night her mother died that way.

Not daring to probe any deeper for fear of the Agency getting sued, she'd considered reaching out to Becker.

No, Fanuzzi might answer the phone, and she couldn't deal with that right now.

After the waitress refilled her coffee and took away her dishes, Miranda pulled her laptop closer on the table.

So what was the next step?

She stared at the screen, willing the answer to appear. C'mon. Think.

If Leon left that sponge on the stair, he'd have to know her mother's schedule. When she'd be pulling pills, when she'd be going from floor three to floor two. He'd have to know she was working a double shift that night.

He'd have to get the timing just right, too, or someone else might have stepped on that sponge.

He might have asked one of the nurses for information, but he would have drawn suspicion.

So that left observation.

It probably took him weeks to learn everything he needed to know. He might have gone to her mother's house and followed her to work. He might have even followed her inside the hospital. Once he knew she was in the Neuro unit, he could come back at will and discover her habits, which were pretty routine.

Maybe somebody noticed him.

So who would have seen a cop wandering the halls of the hospital—and remember it seventeen years later? Alice hadn't mentioned him.

Cops visited hospitals from time to time. To interview a witness or a victim.

Maybe no one took any notice of him. No, there had to be somebody.

She sat up. Of course. That cleaning man. Surely he would have spotted Leon snooping around the floor. He was supposed to have been her mother's friend.

But where was that guy? He'd been dismissed seventeen years ago. He might be impossible to locate now.

Wait a minute. What was the dude's name? She flipped through the Inquiry again. Yontz. Hardwick Yontz.

Expecting to find nothing, she typed the name into her laptop.

To her shock, it came up right away. Yontz Commercial Cleaning. On Roosevelt Road. Had to be him. Right? She'd find out.

Gulping down the last swallow of coffee, she packed up her laptop, paid the bill, and headed out.

She was going to pay this Mr. Yontz a visit and ask him about Leon herself.

CHAPTER TWENTY-FOUR

Back in her rented Tesla, Miranda headed down Lake Street through downtown Oak Park, with its quaint old world style buildings.

Mid morning traffic was heavier than she expected, and she ended up stopped at a red light behind a delivery van. Craning her neck, she struggled to see how many cars were in front of her.

A lot.

It would take several light changes to get through the intersection. With a grunt, she sat back and tapped her fingers on the steering wheel.

The sky was overcast, and the temperature had dropped to fifty-two. As she waited, a light mist started up. She fiddled with the steering wheel, and the wipers came on. Okay, she figured out that, but where was the heat on this seventeen-inch screen? She poked around some more. Music playlists, energy consumption, GPS. Nothing marked "Heat."

Disgusted with herself, her gaze wandered to the sidewalk.

What in the world?

A long line of people snaked down the sidewalk and around the corner at the end of the block. As umbrellas began to go up, Miranda realized most of them were women. Many were holding something in their arms. A book.

Squinting hard, she only had to make out part of the title. *My Ordeal.*

She leaned over and peered at the store entrance at the front of the line. She looked up at the black awning over the display windows. Then she read the bold white art nouveau lettering on the fabric.

"Booktopia."

Oh, brother.

The light turned and the van in front of her moved up. With a sudden surge of indignation, she squeezed the Tesla into the only open spot along the curb.

Hopping out of the car, Miranda ignored the chill in the air as she hurried to the sidewalk. There she ignored the parking meter—there was no time to dig for change—and wrestled her way up the line to the front door.

"Hey you, get in the back," called a tall woman with long black hair and a shrill voice.

"Yeah, who do you think you are?" said the short woman in front of her.

Miranda turned and gave them a sweet smile. "I'm just getting an Italian cookbook." Almost the same thing she'd said in Saint Simons.

She pushed past the women and through the front door.

The warm air felt good, but now that she was inside, she didn't know why she was doing this. Guess she just had to see it for herself.

The murmurs of the crowd echoed against the store's high-domed ceiling. The place was laid out in a circular design, with the shelves making a star configuration that converged at the center.

That was where the signing was.

Miranda made her way around the bestseller table—which actually did feature Italian cookbooks—and ducked down the first row. She tiptoed past the shelves of romance novels to the end of the aisle and peeked out.

And there they were, just like in Saint Simons.

In a glittery gold top, a thick gold necklace around her neck, and long gold earbobs dangling from her lobes, Audrey Wilson sat at the table with a big "I'm a celebrity" grin, drinking in the adoration of her fans.

She'd had her hair cut, and wore a headful of thick, golden chin-length curls.

So the book tour for her best seller, *My Ordeal*, had made it all the way to Oak Park, Illinois. Whoopie.

And just as predictable was Curt Holloway.

He stood next to Audrey, still playing bodyguard, and he looked totally starstruck.

Ugh. Miranda was so mad at Holloway, she could spit. He'd been her colleague. He'd saved her life once. She'd saved his. They weren't always on the same page. He'd never liked her being in charge, but she didn't want to see him ruin his career.

Not for the likes of Audrey Wilson.

Same as before, the uniformed real bodyguard from Audrey's prison stood behind them, blending into the background of books. Holloway should let that guy take over and hop the next flight back to Atlanta.

A fan stepped up to the table, and with a smile as big as Audrey's, Holloway handed Audrey a glittery pen. So he was playing bodyguard and helper to the star.

Someone else handed Audrey a copy of *My Ordeal* from a stack on the table. Miranda couldn't see the person for the fan.

Audrey opened the book, scrawled something on a page, and handed the copy to the fan. "I hope you enjoy it, Katie."

The fan's gushing voice echoed up to the ceiling. "Oh, I know I will. Thank you. Thank you so much."

The woman scampered away, hugging the book to her chest and giving Miranda a clear view of the man sitting next to Audrey.

Deep black, gel-laden hair, pinstripe suit, big oily smile, full of himself. Miranda wouldn't exactly call him handsome, but she bet he would.

And from the eyelashes Audrey was batting at him, she would, too.

Holloway bent down to gently rub Audrey's wrist. "Are you getting tired?"

The man at the table took her other hand. "She's fine. She's a trooper. Right, sweetheart?"

Holloway looked crestfallen.

Sweetheart?

But Audrey shook them both off and turned to the next person in line, her smile bigger than ever.

She was really enjoying the attention. From everyone.

Movement caught Miranda's eye.

A tall thin woman stood at the end of an aisle of books two rows behind the signing table. The shoulders of her dark suit bobbed up and down as she quietly sobbed into a tissue. Her makeup was a mess, but there wasn't a short white-blond hair on her head out of place.

Gen.

Again? Still?

What was she doing here? Yesterday morning Gen had been in Miranda's office going over reports.

Miranda thought back over the last week or so. Gen had been out last Tuesday. Friday she'd left early saying she had a dental appointment.

Had that been a fib? Had Gen been following Audrey's itinerary, showing up at her signings just to moon over Holloway?

That was disgusting.

Gen was better than that. Miranda wanted to shake some sense into the girl. She should have gotten over Holloway a long time ago. He'd dumped her for his ex-wife, for Pete's sake.

And then she spotted someone else standing at the end of the aisle where the bookshelves curved, giving him a perfect view of both Holloway and Gen. He was pretending to read a spy novel, but Miranda could see he had his eye on Gen. And that he wore the same lovestruck look on his baby face he had in Saint Simons.

Alex Witherby.

Parker still had him watching Holloway? Or maybe he was here on his own to watch Gen.

Either way, Miranda wanted to shake him, too.

She'd had enough.

She spun around, headed back down the aisle of books and around the back to the one where she'd seen Witherby standing.

Stepping into the aisle, she saw he hadn't moved.

She rushed up behind and tapped him on his linebacker shoulder.

He jumped, which looked strange for such a big guy, and he nearly dropped his book. Then he turned around and stared at her with his pale blue eyes, jaw hanging open.

Miranda smirked at him. "Didn't see me this time, did you, Witherby?"

Witherby found his tongue. "Ms. Steele. Wha—what are you doing in Chicago?"

"Oak Park is a suburb of Chicago."

Witherby was still too stunned to answer.

"You should talk to her," Miranda said softly.

"What?" he whispered back.

She waved a hand toward the far aisle. "Gen. You should talk to her."

Witherby looked back over his shoulder and realized Miranda had caught him staring at Gen.

His pale cheeks turning pink, he folded his arms over his bulky chest. "You were mistaken in Saint Simons, Ms. Steele. I do not have the 'hots' for Mr. Parker's daughter."

What a formal denial.

Miranda folded her arms. "I am a private investigator, you know."

Witherby scowled.

"But it wouldn't take a private investigator to figure it out."

Witherby's shoulders slumped.

She made a helpless gesture. "So instead of you both standing here being miserable, go talk to her."

Witherby blinked at her in shock. "I—I wouldn't know what to say."

"Ask her out for coffee or something."

"She wouldn't go with someone like me."

He had a point, but Miranda hadn't thought Gen would fall for someone like Holloway, either. "You'll never know unless you try." It was all the advice she could think of.

For a moment, she could see the wheels turn in Witherby's head as he imagined himself across from Gen at a table in some cozy Java hut.

Then he shook his head. "She'd just laugh at me."

Miranda felt like butting the stubborn guy with her head. He might be a big bulky football player type bodyguard, but when it came to Gen, he was a creampuff.

"Suit yourself." And she threw up her hands, spun on her heels, and headed back up the aisle and out of the store.

What was she doing here playing Yenta anyway when she had a case to solve?

She had to find her mother's killer.

CHAPTER TWENTY-FIVE

Outside, Miranda climbed back into the Tesla and pulled off, glad at least she hadn't been booted for not feeding the parking meter.

Her head was still pounding from frustration over the lovelorn trio in the bookstore, but when she calmed down and looked out her windshield, she could feel her luck changing.

The rain had stopped, the sun had come out, and the traffic had thinned. It took Miranda only twenty minutes to get to Yontz Commercial Cleaning.

The place turned out to be a modest storefront with a plain dark brown awning wedged into a block-long beige brick building. Better feed the meter this time.

As she sat digging change out of her pocket, Miranda wondered what she would do if she did learn Leon had killed her mother.

He was already dead.

The knowledge she had made him that way didn't seem like enough payback. But maybe Aunt Lu would be happy.

And then, a trickle of fear worked its way up her spine. What if she was wrong about Leon? What if Yontz, the cleaning man who was supposed to have been her mother's friend, was the real killer?

Either way, she had to know.

Determined to find out the truth, she shook off her nerves, hopped out of the Tesla, stuffed her coins into the meter, and marched inside the office.

She found herself in a spotless reception area that smelled of antiseptic.

The walls were a clean pale beige. The gray LVT floor was immaculate. Several empty sky blue chairs were arranged around a table where copies of *Business Weekly* and *Golf Digest* lay.

A video played on a TV in the corner. On the screen Miranda watched a tall guy with a long mop cleaning a bathroom.

"Mop in a consistent figure-eight pattern," said a generic-sounding narrator. "Use overlapping strokes and turn the mop head often."

Training video.

But no one was here to see it.

Across from the seating area stood a light-colored counter with a plexiglass partition.

No one was behind it.

Miranda strolled over to the counter and looked at the brochures sitting in a holder. A picture of the same dude with the mop was on the cover along with the company logo.

"Professional, committed industry leader. Want the best? You want Yontz."

She wanted him, alright. She wanted him to give her answers.

Wishing for a bell to ring, she stood on tiptoe to see if someone was crouched behind the desk. Her nose was just about to touch the glass partition when a door in the back opened and a musical voice rang out.

"Yes, Ms. Gorski. We can have a team out to your office tonight. Yes, of course. As you know, we send out only the best, most dedicated people."

Her heels tapping over the super-clean floor, a middle-aged, copper skinned woman in a navy skirt and crimson jacket came through the door and headed to the desk.

Under a chic crop of black-and-bronze hair, she wore an earbud, and in one hand she carried a tablet, which she punched at with tapered silver fingernails.

"I'm booking you right now," she said in a customer-friendly voice.

Miranda's stomach sank. This woman looked like she ran this business. Must be a relative. If she were lucky.

The woman hung up, slid her tablet into a holder on the desk, and turned to her with a smile. "May I help you?"

Miranda picked up a brochure. "I'd like to speak to—"

"If you're looking for professional cleaning services, you've found the best. No need to look any further."

In addition to running the business, she was a pushy salesperson. "Actually, I'm looking for someone named Hardwick Yontz. Does he work here?"

The woman's friendly smile grew just a bit tight. "Mr. Yontz isn't available right now. I assure you I can answer any questions you might have."

"You mean Mr. Yontz does work here?"

"Of course, he does. He's the owner."

The owner. Just like she'd thought in the first place. And this woman wasn't. But Miranda would have to get through her to get to Yontz. She dug for a card in her pocket and handed it to the woman.

"My name is Miranda Steele. I'm a private investigator looking into a cold case. I think Mr. Yontz may have some relevant information."

The woman blinked at her. "A cold case?"

"It involves a suspicious death."

She studied the card. Before she could come up with another excuse, the side door opened again and a man stuck his head inside the area. "Delilah,

Arnold says he can't get to the job you assigned him this afternoon. He's got car trouble."

The woman rolled her eyes. "Not again."

The man spotted Miranda and stepped inside the area behind the counter, letting the door close behind him. He was tall and thin, dressed in gray Chinos and a light blue polo shirt with the Yontz logo on the pocket. He had a longish face, high cheekbones, and a mustache that was turning gray. His neck was thin, his face was lined, and his hair was cut short, but she could see it was mostly gray, too. Her mother would have been almost sixty, so he seemed to be the right age.

"Are you Hardwick Yontz?" Miranda said.

The woman behind the counter glared at her as if Miranda needed her permission to speak to this guy.

Ignoring the woman's reaction, the man turned to Miranda with kind, deep brown eyes. "I am. Who do we have here?"

"This woman claims to be a private investigator. She says she's on a cold case. She wants to talk to you about it." Everything in her tone said, "Get rid of her," but she handed Yontz Miranda's card anyway.

Yontz took it and stared down at it for a long moment. His kind face took on an odd expression. Miranda watched the emotions play over his features.

Shock. Concern. Disbelief.

This was the guy, alright. The cleaning man who had been her mother's friend. And maybe her killer.

He looked up at her again, his eyes glowing with amazement. "Miranda Steele? Hilda Steele's daughter?"

Bingo. "That's correct."

The woman drew in an anxious breath. "Is this about what I think it is, Hardwick?"

Miranda steadied her gaze on Yontz. "It's about what happened to my mother seventeen years ago."

"Don't talk to her. I'll call our lawyer."

Hardwick raised a large hand. "You'll do no such thing, Delilah. I had nothing to hide seventeen years ago, and I have nothing to hide now. I'd be happy to talk to you, Ms. Steele. Just let me buzz you in."

CHAPTER TWENTY-SIX

Yontz disappeared, and a moment later a buzzer sounded, and another door next to the sitting area opened.

He beckoned her with his hand and a warm smile as if she were a long lost friend. "C'mon in."

She stepped through the opening and let him lead her through a corridor to a large room in the back.

The antiseptic smell was stronger here, and the space was filled with boxes of supplies. Gloves, goggles, cleaning rags, paper towels, brushes, mop heads. A few vacuum cleaners stood in a corner, and several bottles of fluid sat on a wire shelf behind a U-shaped laminate desk that held an open laptop and piles of papers.

Yontz took a folding chair that was leaning next to the vacuum cleaners and opened it for her.

"Sorry about the accommodations. Delilah deals with the customers. I do the books and supervise the employees. Don't need anything fancy for that."

Guess not. Miranda perched on the seat. "Is Delilah your daughter?"

Yontz let out a low musical laugh. "Lord, no. She's my wife. She wears her age better than I do. Though she is several years younger than me." He reached for a carafe that sat on a small cabinet in the far corner.

Miranda had just noticed the smell of fresh-brewed coffee chasing away the cleaner odor.

"Would you like some?"

She'd already had too much in the restaurant, but saying no might make him clam up. "Sure. Thanks."

He took a cup from a tray next to the coffee machine and poured. The cup was red with white lettering that said, "Keep Calm and Clean Up."

"Cream and sugar?"

"Plain."

He handed the steaming cup to her.

"Thanks." She took a sip.

It was pretty good, she decided, as Yontz refilled a cup on his desk. It was shiny blue with white lettering that read, "Best Boss Ever."

She couldn't help wondering if Delilah had given it to him, but this man was so warm and friendly, he probably was a good boss. Miranda couldn't imagine what a conversation between him and her mother would have sounded like. And right now, she couldn't imagine him killing her, either.

She hoped she wasn't wrong.

Yontz returned the carafe to its place, went around his desk, and sat down in a squeaky office chair. Leaning back, he studied her in silence.

Finally he said, "So you're Hilda's little girl."

Miranda felt as if she were dressed in her underwear. She couldn't imagine what this man might know about her. Straightening her back, she cleared her throat. "I'm here in a professional capacity, Mr. Yontz."

"Oh, please call me Hardwick."

Uncomfortable with the friendliness, Miranda shifted her weight on the hard metal of her seat. "I need to ask you some questions about my mother's accident."

A corner of his lip turned up. "You come straight to the point, don't you. Hilda was like that, too."

He sounded like Alice Whitaker.

"It's been a long time, but I sure do miss her. I know you do, too." His look was knowing, and Miranda wondered if he might be trying to get information out of her, too. "I worked with her for many years. I considered her a friend."

"So I understand."

"I admired her."

They were getting off track. She set her cup on his desk. "Mr. Yontz—"

"Hardwick." He smiled and took a swallow of coffee.

"Hardwick. Suburban General Hospital conducted an investigation after my mother's accident seventeen years ago. Are you aware of their findings?"

He sat back in his chair. "Hard not to be. They kicked me out."

"They said you accidentally dropped the sponge on the stairs. The one my mother slipped on."

Yontz narrowed his eyes at her. "That's what they claimed."

"And were they wrong?"

His gaze said the answer was obvious.

Maybe she should go about this a little less directly. She reached for her cup again. "You must feel a lot of resentment toward the hospital for letting you go."

He chuckled. "Lord, no. Leaving there was the best thing that ever happened to me. I'll admit I was down in the mouth for a good long while, had to take an odd job here and there. Then I met Delilah, and she kept telling me I should go to work for myself. Finally I decided that was a good idea. We got a license, started Yontz Commercial Cleaning, and we never looked back. We make more with this business than I ever could have at the hospital."

With another warm smile, he turned to the photos on the wall. "We put two kids through college. They were Delilah's from a previous marriage, but I adopted them. Our son's a lawyer in New York. Our daughter is a marketing director at a manufacturing firm downtown. We have five grandkids who are all in college. So, no, I have no resentment."

Miranda wasn't sure what to say to all that.

"You know, your mother used to encourage me to go out on my own, too. She said I was better than that hospital job. I only wish she could have lived to see this place."

Miranda was still having a hard time envisioning her mother as a confidant. And what Yontz just described certainly wasn't the curriculum vitae of a man who had committed murder. He was innocent.

She needed more information. She put her cup down again. "Back to that investigation. Do you know anyone else on the hospital staff who might have put the sponge on the stair on purpose?"

Instead of answering, Yontz sat back and folded his arms.

What was he hiding? "Let me ask you this. Did you happen to see a policeman hanging around the floors where my mother worked back then?"

He frowned. "A policeman?"

"Someone in uniform. Dark hair, narrow eyes, kinda mean."

"Are you talking about Leon Groth?"

Miranda was stunned he knew the name. And remembered it after all these years. "You knew Leon Groth?"

"Your mother used to talk to me about him. Said he was no good. Said you married him to get away from her. She was real sorry about that."

The same thing Alice had told her. Again Miranda felt the same gut punch. But Yontz didn't seem to know about how her mother had threatened Leon.

Suppressing the wave of emotions from that revelation, Miranda pressed on. "So you would have recognized Groth if he'd been hanging around the hospital?"

Yontz sat back and rubbed his chin. "I knew the name. I recognized it when that story came out about how he died in Lake Placid a while back. I was glad you weren't with him any longer. Hilda would have been relieved, too."

Miranda reached for her cup again and used the coffee to swallow down another shockwave. And here she didn't think she could despise being in the news any more than she already did.

But at least Yontz was giving her something. "And you never saw Groth on the Neuro floors in the hospital?"

"No, I didn't."

"Are you sure?" This wasn't the answer she'd been expecting.

"I would remember if he had been there. Like your mother, I worked a lot of double shifts. I kept my eyes open."

Her theory was falling apart. "Mr. Yontz, I have reason to believe Leon Groth might have wanted my mother dead. Do you think there was any way he could have put the sponge on the stair?"

He shook his head. "No, I don't."

He seemed very sure of that answer. He knew something. "What do you think happened, then?"

His face took on a faraway look. "I've thought about that night for a long time. I've gone over and over it in my mind, and I keep coming up with the same idea."

"What idea?"

Hesitating, he tapped his long fingers on some papers on his desk.

She had to make him talk. "Mr. Yontz, the hospital's inquiry report included your interview."

He sat up, surprised. "You read that report?"

"The CEO gave it to me. You were asked about that sponge."

"Yes, I was."

"You started to answer, and the interviewer cut you off."

"Yes, he did."

"What were you going to say?"

"I was going to tell him how I knew for certain I didn't drop that sponge."

Her stomach tightened. "How?"

His deep brown eyes glowing with intensity, he leaned forward. "Because the cleaning crew never used sponges. Too much cross contamination."

Now it was Miranda's turn to sink back into her chair. Once again, she felt like she'd been hit in the chest with a rock. The cleaning crew didn't use sponges? How could that Inquiry be so off base?

Finally she caught her breath. "Then someone else put that sponge there. Who?"

Yontz drew in a breath through his nose. "Like I said, I've thought about the night your mother died for a long time."

"And?"

"And there's one thing I just can't shake."

She waited.

"Hilda was having a problem with one of the surgeons on the floor."

She didn't expect that answer. "What kind of a problem?"

"Hilda didn't want to say. She didn't want me to get into trouble. At first I let it go, but then one night a few weeks later, she was so upset she told me."

"Upset about what?"

"She said she had to change the dosage for the meds for one of that surgeon's patients. Pain meds. Narcotics. It was way too high. She had to get another doctor to sign off on it. He'd given her a hard time, told her one of the other nurses must have entered the wrong dosage, but Hilda knew that surgeon had done it."

No wonder she was mad.

"Then there was the time she found that same surgeon in a patient's room messing with the IV."

"Was that unusual?"

"It wasn't his patient."

"What did she think? That the surgeon was incompetent?" A scary idea.

"She didn't use that word, but she told me she was thinking about reporting him to the higher-ups."

"And did she?"

"I don't know. But the night of her accident, we both worked a double shift. 'Bout an hour before midnight, I heard Hilda arguing in that surgeon's office. They were shouting at each other."

Uh oh.

"Just after the midnight shift started, I caught up with her. Told her I'd overheard the argument. I warned her she was playing with fire. She got mad at me. We had words. Finally, she said I should mind my own business and walked away."

That was the "bickering" Alice Whitaker had overheard.

"It was the last thing she said to me." Yontz grew suddenly silent and stared down at his coffee cup, lost in the sadness of the past.

Miranda was wishing she'd had better final memories of her mother, too. But she still didn't have all the answers she needed.

"Mr. Yontz, I'm not sure what you're saying."

"Like I said, the cleaning crew never used sponges."

"Okay."

"But surgeons do."

"It was a *surgical* sponge on the stairs?"

"Nobody ever said. But I think it had to be."

And the hospital covered that up. "Did my mother ever tell you the name of the surgeon?"

"Not at first, but she did later on. That was how I knew what she was arguing about in his office that night."

"And who was it?"

Yontz nodded. "He was a neurosurgeon. His name was Dr. Bogart E. Musgrove."

Miranda nearly gasped out loud. "Dr. Bogart E. Musgrove?"

"That's right."

Feeling shaky, she could barely get out the next words. "He was the one who signed my mother's death certificate."

Yontz's voice turned dark as a storm. "And he was the one who found her on the stairwell that night."

CHAPTER TWENTY-SEVEN

Miranda didn't remember how she drove the seven miles back to Suburban General Hospital. All she knew was that she was determined to have it out with that lying CEO.

"You can't go in there," the administrative assistant warned her as she approached her desk.

Ignoring her, Miranda barreled past the assistant and burst through the office door without bothering to knock.

"We need to talk, Williamson."

At his desk, Bryant Williamson jumped, nearly knocking over his open laptop, and gaped up at her in bewilderment. It took him only a second to recover and turn to the others in the room.

In his teal blue guest chairs sat two men and a woman, all in suits, holding tablets and scowling at her.

Williamson cleared his throat and straightened his tie. "Let's move this meeting to Conference Room C," he said to the group. Then he addressed his screen. "Janet, Frank, I'll call you back in a few minutes." He clicked out of whatever window they were in.

After everyone shuffled out, he turned to Miranda looking very annoyed. "Now that you've disrupted our budget meeting, what can I do for you, Ms. Steele?"

Miranda marched over to his desk, put her palms on it, and got in his face. "Where is Dr. Musgrove?"

"Dr. Musgrove?"

"Dr. Bogart E. Musgrove. The doctor who signed my mother's death certificate. The doctor who found my mother in the stairwell. The doctor who probably put that sponge on the stair. The one she slipped on? Remember?"

With a look of pain, Williamson closed his eyes and let out a sigh. "I might have known that inquiry report wouldn't satisfy you. It didn't satisfy me when I first read it, either."

That response surprised her. "Answer my question. Where's Dr. Musgrove?"

"I don't know."

"What do you mean, you don't know?"

"Please have a seat." His face said he was ready to talk and he had a lot to say, so she complied.

As she pulled up one of the teal-blue chairs, Williamson got up, closed the door, and headed back to his desk, looking like he was carrying the weight of the world on his shoulders.

She almost felt sorry for him.

He sat down and put his head in his hands. He needed prompting.

"So you knew that inquiry report you gave me yesterday was bogus?"

He made a sour face. "I wouldn't use that word, but I knew the hospital's investigation was incomplete.

"Incomplete?"

"It had holes in it."

"Like Swiss cheese."

He coughed. "That's one way of putting it."

"If you weren't satisfied with the report, why didn't you continue the investigation?"

He frowned at her. "I wasn't here then."

Miranda blinked. She hadn't realized that.

"I came into this position about a year after my predecessor resigned. He was the one who ordered the inquiry."

"Okay." So Williamson wasn't directly responsible for it. Or for Dr. Musgrove.

Shaking his head, he stared out the window. "Being the CEO of a prominent medical facility might seem like a gravy job to some, but it's far from it. You're responsible for overseeing operating policies and procedures, budgeting, staffing, as well as strategic planning for the facility and regulatory compliance. You have to balance the needs of the staff and the patients. You have to keep up with technological changes in the industry. You have to be excellent at budgeting as well as handling people. You have to continually nurture the hospital's relationships in the community. Unfortunately my predecessor—let's just say he wasn't up to all that."

"He wasn't fit for the job?"

"He was on paper."

"What do you mean?"

Williamson picked up a pen and turned it over in his hand. "My predecessor graduated from Harvard with honors. He came from a wealthy family. His parents knew several board members and donated generously to Suburban General. They thought the position was perfect for him."

Miranda scowled. "He was given the job."

"I don't know about that. All I know is that from the state things were in when I came on board, the responsibilities must have overwhelmed him."

"And so?"

"And so the hospital suffered. We were short-staffed and ill supplied. And there was a lack of due diligence in some of our processes."

Miranda thought about what Alice Whitaker had said about the working conditions when her mother was here.

"He resigned about a year after the incident with your mother."

He was gone. "Where is he now?" She'd like to rake him over the coals.

"He passed away about five years ago."

She slumped in her chair. But she wasn't done. "One of the people interviewed in the hospital's inquiry was Hardwick Yontz from the cleaning crew."

"Yes."

"He denied dropping the sponge on the stairs the night my mother died."

"Yes."

"The interviewer cut him off."

With an expression of disgust, Williamson nodded in agreement. "That was one of the problems I had with the report."

But she knew more than what was in that report now. "A little while ago I talked to Hardwick Yontz."

Williamson sat up. "You are a good investigator. How—how is he?"

"He's doing well. Owns his own cleaning business."

"That's good to hear."

She saw palpable guilt on the CEO's face, even though he wasn't responsible for getting Yontz dismissed.

"I asked him how he could be so sure he didn't drop that sponge. Do you know what he said?"

Williamson narrowed his eyes. "Because the cleaning crew didn't use sponges. Sponges are used by surgeons in the operating rooms."

Miranda drew in a breath. "You knew that?"

"Most people working on the floors would know that."

"And yet no one on the board questioned it."

Williamson nodded. "Mr. Yontz was obviously the scapegoat."

"Why him?"

He shrugged. "He was an easy target. The medical staff has access to the operating rooms. They're in charge of cleaning them. Anyone who worked in there might have taken that sponge. If the committee questioned everyone, my guess is they feared it would cause mistrust and possibly a loss of personnel on a floor that was already short-staffed."

Miranda leaned toward the CEO. "But it wasn't just anyone. Yontz told me my mother had a problem with Dr. Musgrove. He said she caught him overdosing patients. He said she was going to file a complaint against him."

Williamson's expression turned hard. "She did."

"Did she?"

"I discovered it when I looked into the matter. I also learned that though he was an excellent surgeon, Dr. Musgrove lost an unusual number of patients while he was here."

Unusual number? "What do you mean?"

"Three of Dr. Musgrove's patients had a good prognosis after surgery. But then—"

"What?"

"Something went wrong. All of them died. Later, it was discovered each of them had been given a high dose of pain medication. More than they could tolerate."

Miranda's chest began to burn. "They were overdosed. It was Dr. Musgrove who gave them that medication. That's why my mother reported him. Why wasn't something done?"

"Records weren't the best back then. Apparently it was easy to blame someone else for the dosage. It seems Dr. Musgrove could be quite intimidating. No one wanted to say he was responsible for the death of those patients. There wasn't enough solid proof to prosecute. If the administration had tried and failed, Dr. Musgrove might have sued the hospital."

Couldn't have that. "So nothing happened to him?"

"He was dismissed about a year after the incident with your mother."

She couldn't believe it. He just walked away free and clear? "Dismissed? Where did he go?"

"A small hospital in Cedar Rapids."

Cedar Rapids? That was a couple hundred miles away in the next state. "Is he still there? Overdosing patients?"

"No. I wrote to the Executive Director there when I looked into the inquiry and conducted my own research. I sent her my findings on Dr. Musgrove and recommended he be sanctioned. He was dismissed from Cedar River after about a year."

So Williamson had some guts. He wasn't the bad guy here. He was trying to fix the mess his predecessor had left. Writing to that hospital must have saved lives. Unless Musgrove was practicing elsewhere.

Her stomach clenched with anxiety, Miranda fixed the CEO with a hard gaze. "Mr. Williamson, where is Dr. Musgrove now?"

Williamson looked more filled with regret than ever as he raised his hands in a helpless gesture. "I have no idea."

CHAPTER TWENTY-EIGHT

Miranda paced back and forth in her hotel suite, feeling as if she were on fire.

Coming to a halt in front of the tall windows, she pressed her hands to her face. Her temples throbbed. Her stomach was so tight she felt sick. She shivered with shock as everything she'd learned that morning rolled through her brain again.

Hardwick Yontz couldn't have killed her mother because the cleaning crew didn't use sponges. But the neurosurgeon her mother was having it out with did. Her mother had discovered that guy was giving patients overdoses of pain meds and reported him to the hospital administration.

Miranda could just imagine her mother marching into his office and telling him she was going to report him.

"Medicine isn't fun and games," she probably told him.

This Dr. Musgrove was intimidating, Williamson had said, but he hadn't intimidated her mother.

And then her mother had conveniently slipped on a sponge going down a stairwell.

A stairwell Dr. Musgrove knew she would take. And a sponge that came from the operating room he worked in.

But the hospital covered it up, and the surgeon wasn't questioned. Meanwhile, several of his patients died from his overdosing.

It all made Miranda's blood boil.

She was convinced it was Dr. Musgrove who killed her mother, but she needed closure. She needed a confession. And if this guy was still overdosing patients somewhere, she needed to stop him.

Right now, all she knew was that she had to find this Dr. Bogart E. Musgrove.

But how? He was in the wind.

Before she left the hospital, Williamson had given her all he had on Musgrove, and she now had papers spread over the desk and files up on her laptop.

Williamson had done his research.

Pouring herself yet another cup of coffee, which she'd made in the hotel suite's complimentary machine, she sat down and read over the documents one more time.

Bogart Elrod Musgrove had grown up in Doncaster, Indiana, a small town about thirty miles west of Indianapolis. In high school, his grades were good, he was a regular on the honor roll, he even played on the football team. Seemed like an all-round normal kid. If it weren't for what Williamson had included in the folder on her desk.

She opened it and looked over the newspaper clippings and internet printouts on Musgrove.

There was a photo of Musgrove at seventeen.

With the football field and the scoreboard in the background, he stood with his hands behind his back in his blue-and-white uniform, the number thirty-eight proudly displayed across his chest. His dark wavy hair was cut in a messy style parted down the middle. Thick dark brows were spaced evenly over large dark eyes. His lips were thin, and he wore no smile. His look was hollow, as if he wasn't really there. And with the black marks under his eyes, he seemed eerily menacing.

The article told her he was smallish for a linebacker. Five foot eleven and one-ninety, though the shoulder pads made him look bigger than he was.

He must have been strong.

In a game in the middle of the season, Musgrove's high school had played against a longtime rival. In the fourth quarter, Musgrove's team was ahead twenty-four to seven, even though the quarterback on the rival team had prospects for college and a promising career as a professional player.

According to the article, after the whistle blew, Musgrove sacked the quarterback, slamming him to the ground with all his weight. Referees had to pull Musgrove off the kid.

Turned out the quarterback's leg was badly broken from the tackle, ruining his hopes for a college scholarship.

To everyone who saw it, the attack seemed intentional.

"When the linebacker got up, there was glee on his face," said one of the parents.

"Do you think Musgrove had a vendetta against that quarterback?" a reporter asked a classmate who claimed to know the player.

"You mean like a grudge? Naw. He just likes mowing folks down."

"He's a bully."

"Yeah, that's the word I'd use."

Apparently he'd done that a lot on the field, though this was the worst incident.

Sounded like he had a lot of pent up anger. About what, Miranda couldn't tell. There was no information about his mother or a girlfriend.

Another article was clipped behind the football story. This one was about the lawsuit the quarterback's parents brought against Musgrove.

A year later, a judge dismissed the case. The article speculated that Musgrove's father, a prominent lawyer in the town, was a friend of the judge, and because of that, he was biased. There was no proof, and neither Musgrove suffered any repercussions from the accusation.

So the younger Musgrove was used to getting away with things because Daddy would bail him out.

Miranda returned to Williamson's summary on her screen.

After high school, Musgrove attended the state university. Apparently he immersed himself in his studies and did not participate in any sports programs. Four years later, he graduated with honors with an undergraduate degree. He continued in the medical division, completing the MD-PhD and neurosurgery residency program fifteen years later. He was forty when he started working at Suburban General in Oak Park. About the same age her mother had been at the time.

The summary ended with the information about Cedar River Medical Center that Williamson had already told her and a copy of the letter he'd sent to the person in charge there.

Miranda sat back and ran her hands through her hair as she thought again about her mother confronting Musgrove and reporting him to the higher-ups.

That had taken real guts. Miranda couldn't help admiring her. Not a feeling she ever would have expected to have toward her mother.

Another seismic shift.

And so this Dr. Musgrove planned to kill her mother to shut her up. He knew her schedule, or could easily learn it. All he had to do was grab a sponge from the operating room, and when the time was right, slip into the restroom, wet the sponge, go to the stairwell, and put it on the first step.

All without being seen. And without dripping water on the floor. Maybe he used a basin or something.

But why was Musgrove over medicating his patients? Was he incompetent? He seemed too smart for that. Was he killing them on purpose? Was he a cold-blooded serial killer?

If he was, and nobody had enough proof to stop him, he was probably still out there somewhere overdosing people.

She had to find him. Somebody at the Cedar Rapids hospital had to know something, she decided.

Determined to get to that person, Miranda reached for her phone and dialed the contact number at the end of Williamson's summary.

Then she sat back in disgust as a friendly recorded voice came on the line. "Thank you for calling Cedar River Medical Center. If this is an emergency, hang up and dial 911."

Miranda scowled at the phone. It might be, but 911 couldn't help.

"Your call is very important to us."

Sure it was. That's why she had to listen to a robot.

"If you know your party's extension, enter it now."

Miranda squinted at the screen and punched in the four-digit number for the Executive Director.

"Please hold while we connect you to your party."

Music played. An instrumental version of an old Barry Manilow song.

Miranda tapped her fingers on the desk.

After about four minutes, a pleasant voice came on the line. "Administration."

A real person? Imagine that. "Yes. Hello. Is this, uh," she reached for her laptop and scrolled to the top of the letter. "Is this Gillian Swanson?"

There was a pause. "I'm sorry. Ms. Swanson isn't with us any longer."

Miranda's shoulders slumped. Just her luck. Now what? She needed to find someone who had known Musgrove.

"Can I help you?" asked the voice.

"Are you the new Executive Director?" That person would be familiar with Williamson's letter, right?

"No, I'm her assistant, Ms. Copeland."

Might as well give it a try. "Ms. Copeland, I'm a private investigator, and I'm looking for someone who used to work for Cedar River Medical Center."

"Oh?"

"He was a neurosurgeon. His name is Dr. Bogart Elrod Musgrove."

No reaction to the name. "I see. How long ago did he work here?"

"About fifteen or sixteen years ago."

Probably longer than Ms. Copeland had been there.

"Oh. Well, you would have to speak to someone in HR for that. Let me transfer you."

"There was a letter—"

Barry Manilow again.

Miranda cussed under her breath. She didn't need generic HR records. She needed someone who knew something about this guy.

At least this time the wait wasn't so long.

"Cedar River Medical Center. Human Resources," said another friendly voice before the song got to the chorus. "How can I help you?"

Okay, she'd try again. Start with the obvious, then dig for the dirt. She put on an equally friendly voice. "Hi. My name is Miranda Steele. I'm a private investigator, and I'm looking for information about someone who used to work for you."

"A private investigator?" The woman sounded surprised. And unsure of herself. Maybe she was new.

"I'm wondering if you can confirm that a Dr. Bogart Elrod Musgrove worked for you sixteen years ago."

"Sixteen years ago? Uh..." There was the sound of typing, and then a muffled voice in the background. "Oh, that's right. I'm sorry. I'll have to transfer you to Archives."

"Wait. I just need to ask—"

Barry Manilow one more time. Ugh.

Another five minutes went by. Eight. Ten. Miranda was just about to hang up when someone picked up the phone again.

"Ms. Steele, are you still there?" This was someone different. A woman who sounded older.

"Yes, I'm here."

"I'm Nicole Hutton, the HR Director. Sorry to keep you waiting. I had to check way back in our archives. I can confirm Dr. Bogart Elrod Musgrove worked here in our neurology department for eighteen months."

She gave her the dates. They matched what Williamson had told her.

So far so good. "I understand Dr. Musgrove left under less than desirable circumstances."

There was a pause. "I'm not at liberty to say."

Regulations. "Ms. Hutton, a little while ago, I spoke to Bryant Williamson, the CEO of Suburban General Hospital in Oak Park. He told me all about Dr. Musgrove. In fact, he gave me a copy of everything he sent to your Executive Director, Ms. Swanson."

Silence. Miranda could hear the woman breathing.

Finally, she said, "Then you must know why Dr. Musgrove was dismissed from Cedar River."

Miranda sat up in her chair. Ms. Hutton was confirming Musgrove was let go without saying it directly. "I have an idea. Can I assume there were several unexplained deaths among Dr. Musgrove's patients?"

"You might assume that."

"And that other medical personnel reported overdosing of Dr. Musgrove's patients with pain meds?"

"You might assume that as well." There was bitterness in her tone. She had known Musgrove and was aware of what he had done.

Miranda hoped she knew more. "Do you have any information about where Dr. Musgrove went after he left Cedar River?"

"I'm sorry, I don't."

"A forwarding address? Employment verification from another hospital? Anything?"

There was another long pause, and then the HR Director spoke in a dark tone. "I was here when Dr. Musgrove worked here. I remember him and what he did to our patients. If I knew where he was, I would break the rules and tell you. But I don't know. All I can say is—"

"What?"

"I hope he's in jail."

CHAPTER TWENTY-NINE

Her temples pounding, Miranda stared down at her cell phone.

Dr. Musgrove had murdered his patients. He had to be insane. He had to be a serial killer. Her mother had tried to stop him, and lost her life for it.

She felt dizzy, unable to process her feelings. But she knew that way back then, her mother had felt the same way she would have.

Serial killers didn't stop just because they lost a couple of jobs. She had to find this guy.

But how in the world was she going to do that?

She needed help. She needed her team. She'd bet Becker could find Musgrove. Or at least dig up some more information on him than she had.

For a long moment, she studied her phone, nerves warring in her stomach.

What would she say if Fanuzzi answered? What if she chewed her out again?

It didn't matter.

Downing the rest of her coffee, she inhaled. She had faced serial killers before. And psychos and lunatics.

She could face an angry friend.

She picked up the phone and dialed.

Becker answered on the first ring. "Hey, Steele. Where have you been?"

He didn't sound mad at her. Feeling almost dizzy with relief, she let out her breath. "I'm in Chicago. A suburb. I need your help."

"Oh. Mr. Parker's been out, too. Is he with you?"

Miranda cringed and tried not to think about what kind of trouble Parker might be in. Or what kind of trouble he was in with her. Or that she hadn't heard from him since yesterday. "No, he isn't. Right now I'm looking for somebody. A doctor. It seems he was overdosing some of his patients with pain meds and killing them."

Becker made a choking sound. "He was doing what?"

"Just what I said. Killing his patients."

"Holy moly, Steele. That's unbelievable. That's terrible. That's just—sick. Are the police looking for him, too?"

"The deaths happened over fifteen years ago."

"Oh."

Not that that made the murders any less vicious. "I called the last hospital where he worked. They dismissed him, but nobody knows what happened to him since then."

"And he wasn't arrested?"

"There wasn't enough proof."

"And you need me to get some?"

"I need you to help me find him. If he's at another hospital, there'll be proof." She'd make sure there was. And that it was airtight.

Becker was silent. "Uh oh."

"What? You can help me, can't you?"

"Uh, I'm at home, trying to work, do some laundry, and get some dinner ready for the kids. I have to pick them up from school in a couple of hours. Oh, and I'm in the middle of installing a security suite for Fontana Construction on Peachtree. Doing it remotely. The computer's tied up until it's done."

Was he brushing her off on purpose? "Is there something you want to tell me, Becker?" She braced herself for Becker's version of what Fanuzzi had said to her after her baby shower.

He let out a groan. "I guess there is."

"Does this have to do with Fanuzzi?"

"Yeah."

"Okay, tell me." If Becker hated her as much as Fanuzzi did, she didn't know how she was going to handle it.

But she still needed his skills, and he was still an Agency employee. She only needed him in that capacity. She could keep their relationship professional from now on.

"It's her folks."

"What?"

"Joannie's parents. We've been trying to keep the problems she's been having with the baby from them, but Joannie was in an extra-bad mood the other day when she was on the phone with her mother. She let it slip that she was nauseated. Her mother went nuts. Joannie tried to talk them out of it, but she and Buck are coming in two weeks."

"Buck?"

"Joannie's dad."

Miranda blinked at the phone. This was the last thing she expected Becker to say. "Well, that doesn't sound so bad. You'll have extra help taking care of the kids and running the catering business, won't you?"

"Joannie hates her mother's cooking."

"Oh."

"And it's so crowded. I don't know where we're going to put them. I mentioned getting a bigger house to Joannie, and she nearly bit my head off."

A bigger house? She hadn't told him. Somehow that news gave Miranda hope.

"Yesterday Coco came over with some dishes for the Oglethorpe party, and she said we could all move into the Parker mansion. I was too scared to mention it to Joannie. What do you think? I mean, that's Mr. Parker's family estate."

"I—I think that would be a great idea." She really couldn't process it.

"The thing is—"

"What?"

"Joanie's folks don't care much for me."

"Why? You're a terrific husband."

"Thanks, but that's not how they see it. Joanie told you we were sweethearts in high school, didn't she?"

"Yeah." Miranda recalled Fanuzzi spilling her guts about her past the night she went motorcycle racing down Peachtree Street. "Your family moved away and she ended up with somebody else." Fanuzzi's first husband.

"Right. But did she tell you her parents blamed me for breaking their little girl's heart?"

"No, she didn't."

"Well, they did. They never forgave me."

"How could they blame you? Your folks moved. Besides, you were a kid. You didn't do anything wrong."

"Tell that to them. Maybe when they get here I'll move into my cube at the Agency. A futon should fit in there, don't you think?"

A futon? Becker deserved better than that, but she didn't have time to figure out answers to his family problems right now.

She had to find a killer. "So do you think you can get me something on Dr. Musgrove?"

"Oh, yeah. Right. Okay, send me what you've got on him, and I'll get to it in maybe an hour or two."

An hour or two? "What am I supposed to do until then?"

"I don't know. Try googling him." A loud buzzer went off. "The clothes are done. Gotta go." He hung up.

Miranda scowled at her phone. Googling him?

Well it wasn't a bad idea. One she should have thought of already. This case was too personal. She was losing her touch.

Shaking off the emotions tumbling around inside her like the clothes in Becker's drier, Miranda reached for her keyboard.

Where was this murdering bastard? In ten minutes she had an answer.

Dr. Musgrove had been arrested.

CHAPTER THIRTY

She stared at the text on the screen.

It was an obscure news story from a small town near Peoria, Illinois. An old report from about seven years ago. There was a video. Miranda clicked on it and watched a scruffy-headed man in handcuffs being taken into custody by the local police. Couldn't see his face.

A newswoman's voice explained the scene. "Dr. Bogart Musgrove was arrested two years ago for allegedly feeding his coworkers treats laced with a toxic substance."

He did what?

The video switched to a courtroom.

Wearing a generic suit and tie, with his thick dark hair now trimmed, combed back, and held in place with a lot of gel, Dr. Musgrove rose from the table.

Miranda recognized the same thick brows and dark eyes from his high school football photo. Unnerving.

"How does the defendant plead?" the judge said.

"Guilty, your honor," Musgrove muttered through his thin lips. His voice was meek, but his demeanor told her he was holding back a lot of anger.

"Today Dr. Musgrove was sentenced to five years in prison," said the newsperson. "His colleagues are breathing a sigh of relief."

"I'll bet they were." Miranda read the text beneath the video for more details.

Musgrove had been employed at Hilltop Community Hospital, a hundred-and-thirty bed facility in Peoria with a small neurosurgery division.

How had he gotten that job?

After about a year there, his work had come under scrutiny.

The article didn't say why, but Miranda could guess. During that time, several nurses on his shift became violently ill. It was discovered that they had all eaten treats the doctor had brought into the breakroom. Lab tests confirmed the treats contained arsenic.

Wow. Couldn't make the sponge-on-the-stair thing fly more than once, could you? But this time he didn't get away with it. The HR Director at Cedar Rapids had gotten her wish. Dr. Musgrove went to prison.

Just the idea of that gave Miranda a surge of relief.

Then she spotted an update to the article.

She clicked it. This time the video only showed the exterior of the courthouse. A male voice said, "After serving his sentence, Dr. Bogart Musgrove was released from the State Correctional Center near Peoria, Illinois."

Miranda's stomach sank.

Released.

He'd killed at least three people at Suburban General and more at Cedar River. He got away with it because nobody could prove it. So they let him go free.

He'd been out for over two years. Where was he now?

Still killing people.

Somehow, she knew that in her bones. And somehow she had to find out where he was working.

She forced herself back to the search engine and clicked link after link, reading until the words blurred. There were different spins on the story, more details about the trial, but no new information.

After half an hour, her head was dropping onto the desk.

With a loud grunt of disgust, she got up and shook herself. She stretched, looked around, and realized her stomach was growling.

She ordered a BLT from room service. And more coffee.

When it came, she wolfed it down and read some more. It didn't help. No one knew where Musgrove was. No one had made the connection to Cedar River or Suburban General.

She gritted her teeth in frustration.

Then she spotted a link she hadn't seen before.

"Have you seen this killer?"

She clicked it, expecting an advertisement for male enhancements. Instead, she found a blog. A blog written by one of Musgrove's victims. One of the nurses he'd poisoned at Hilltop Community Hospital.

The last post was only about a year old.

"Warning. Do not hire this doctor," it read. The text talked about the nurse's ordeal and Musgrove's arrest and trial. There were links to the videos Miranda had already watched.

The nurse had photos of Musgrove when he was at Hilltop. One featured a group of doctors in white coats. Musgrove was circled in red. Miranda studied the photo. The man looked like he was the same height he'd been in high school. His dark wavy hair was still parted down the middle. His cheeks were sunken, his chin receding, and his mean look was intensified by those dark features.

She read a few more posts.

The nurse had interviewed the other employees who had been poisoned. Everyone was upset Musgrove had been released. Another nurse insisted this was only the tip of the iceberg.

No further details about that, but the writer seemed to be hinting at something. Had to be careful with a blog or you could get sued.

Miranda read some of the earlier posts. Most of them were rehashes of what she'd said about Musgrove and what she'd been through. Some of them talked about the nursing program at Kankakee Community College. Down at the bottom, Miranda found the blog author's name. Cora Harper. Was she associated with that college?

That she could find out.

She clicked a link to the school Cora had on the sidebar and found the number. Reaching for her phone, she dialed it.

Someone picked up on the first ring. Imagine that. "Administration. How can I direct your call?"

Miranda resisted the urge to cross her fingers for luck. "My name is Miranda Steele, and I'm looking for someone named Cora Harper. Does she work at your school?"

"I'm sorry. I can't give out that information over the phone."

Of course, she couldn't. She should have pretended to be a loan officer verifying employment. "I'm a private investigator, and I need to speak to her about a case I'm looking into."

"Oh? What sort of a case?" The tone was skeptical.

A case involving a serial killer. "It concerns her blog. It's important."

"I can give her a message."

So she did work there. "How soon will she get it?"

"I can't say."

It was the best she could do. "Alright. Tell her I need to speak to her right away. Tell her it's about Dr. Musgrove."

Miranda gave the woman her cell number and hung up.

Her shoulders weary with tension, she put the phone down on the desk with a grimace. Would Cora Harper call her back? Maybe, maybe not. If she was a teacher at the college, she might be busy all afternoon. She might not get the message till tonight. She might not get it until tomorrow morning.

She might not get it at all.

Miranda got up and paced around the suite some more. Should she drive down to that school herself? Right now, she felt sore and headachy and spent. Rubbing her temples, she wandered into the bedroom and studied the bed the hotel staff had neatly made while she was out. A nap sounded wonderful, but she didn't want to miss Cora Harper's call. Or have another nightmare.

She couldn't get down another cup of coffee. Maybe some exercise would help. She was considering hitting the hotel's complimentary gym when her cell rang.

She bolted into the next room and scooped it off the desk. "Hello?"

"Is this Miranda Steele?" said a low cautious voice.

"Yes, it is."

"I'm Cora Harper. I got a message that you had information about Dr. Musgrove?"

Miranda exhaled in relief. "I said I was calling about Dr. Musgrove. I saw your blog, and I wanted to ask you some questions about what happened to you."

No reply.

"Ms. Harper?"

"Everything I know is on my blog. I assume you've already read it?"

"Some of it. But I'm sure there's more to the story."

"Are you a reporter or something?"

"No, I'm a private investigator. I do have some information on Musgrove. I'm wondering if we could get together and compare notes." She needed to talk in person. "I'm in Oak Park now. I can be there in about an hour."

Kankakee was a straight shot down I-75.

"I'm not sure if that's a good idea." She sounded scared.

"Why not?"

Miranda heard her take a deep breath. "It was a long time ago. I'm still trying to get past it."

"I'm sorry for what you went through, Ms. Harper. Maybe it would help if we talked."

"No, it won't. I have to go now."

"Wait. Please, Ms. Harper. I know you're looking for Musgrove. I am, too. Help me find him."

"And why do you care about Dr. Musgrove?"

"I think he killed my mother."

CHAPTER THIRTY-ONE

Cora Harper said yes. A reluctant yes, but a yes.

As fast as she could, Miranda packed up her things, paid her bill, and checked out of the hotel.

Thankfully, the Tesla was fully charged. She maneuvered her way over the surface streets to the Eisenhower, and then through a cluster of other interstates to I-57.

Zooming down the interstate, she flew over the flat asphalt, past dozens of middle class neighborhoods until she reached the wide expanse of land covered by dry grass and corn fields that was the Midwest.

An hour later, she took the off ramp and drove down a quiet street to a small white house with a tiny yard and a cell tower looming in the background. She got out, made her way up the sidewalk to the enclosed porch. All the blinds were shut tight.

Was Ms. Harper even home?

Low laughter came from the sidewalk. Miranda turned and saw two tough looking guys in black leather jackets. They were smoking across the street. Didn't look like the greatest neighborhood in the world.

Ignoring them, she rang the bell.

After what seemed like ten minutes, an inner door opened, footsteps plodded over the porch floor, and a peephole slid open. The person on the other side peered at her a moment, then shut the peephole. Then came the sound of locks being opened. Four of them.

Finally, the first door opened a crack. The screen door was still locked.

A short woman with thick wavy light hair appeared. She was dressed professionally in dark jeans, an ivory blouse with a bow at the neck, and a gray blazer.

She glared at Miranda with a hard look and said nothing.

"Cora Harper?" Miranda asked.

"Who are you?" Her voice was less than gentle.

"I'm Miranda Steele. We spoke on the phone about an hour ago."

She peered over Miranda's shoulder. "Is anybody with you?"

"It's just me." Miranda nodded toward the two dudes who were still loitering on the sidewalk. "If you're worried about those guys across the street, I think we can take them."

Cora Harper's lip turned up for just an instant, then the smile disappeared.

For a moment, Miranda thought she might slam the door in her face.

Instead, she reached for the screen door, turned another lock with a clunk, and pushed it open. "C'mon in. Excuse the mess. I just got home from work."

Miranda stepped inside the porch and waited while Ms. Harper re-latched all the locks.

A gray tabby sat licking its paw on a wicker sofa with a peach cushion. As soon as Ms. Harper opened the inside door, the cat bolted off the seat and into the next room.

"Oh, Newton, what am I going to do with you?"

Shaking her head at the animal, Ms. Harper led her through a small clean kitchen where Newton was scarfing down cat food in a corner. Then they moved into a living room with dark paneling and a dark rug. Dark curtains hung on the windows.

They were pulled shut.

"Have a seat." Switching on a light, Ms. Harper gestured to a worn overstuffed brown couch. "Would you like some lemonade?"

"No, thanks." Cautiously Miranda settled herself onto a cushion, wondering if the thing would hold her. "So you work at the community college?"

The woman nodded. "I teach nursing there."

Probably didn't want to work at a hospital again after what she'd been through.

Ms. Harper sat down in a rocker across from her, picked up a glass from a side table, and sipped it. "Sorry if I sound rude, Ms. Steele. It rattles me to think about that sonofabitch."

"You mean Dr. Musgrove."

"Is there another doctor who likes to poison nurses?"

Miranda hoped not.

"You said you had information on him?"

Miranda shifted her weight. "Before we get to that, why don't you tell me what you know about Musgrove."

"I thought you had read my blog."

"I'd like to hear it in person."

"Okay." Ms. Harper put down her drink and rubbed her hands on her knees. "Musgrove started at Hilltop Community about thirteen years ago. I was the charge nurse on the neuro floor. I remember when he came on board. He wasn't that good-looking, but he was friendly, and very charming."

That wasn't the impression Miranda had gotten of him so far, but someone like that could turn it on when he needed to. "So you'd say he was charismatic?"

She nodded. "That would be the word for it. Everyone liked him at first. We all welcomed him aboard, glad to have another pair of hands. Things went on as usual for about a year or so." She reached for her glass for another sip of lemonade and stared down at the lemon wedge floating in it.

"And then what happened?" Miranda prompted.

Ms. Harper blinked as if coming out of a bad dream. "And then Dr. Musgrove started acting up."

"Acting up?" Miranda had a good idea of what she was talking about.

"I was on the night shift. We had a patient who had had surgery for a ruptured aneurysm the previous morning. Her name was Mrs. Ogden. Dr. Musgrove had performed the procedure. Everything had gone well, and Mrs. Ogden was expected to fully recover. Anyway, I had just stepped into her room to check on her when I saw Dr. Musgrove standing next to her bed in the dark. He had a syringe in his hand and was putting something into her IV. 'What are you doing there, Dr. Musgrove?' I asked. 'There's nothing on the order that she hasn't already been given.' And, boy." Ms. Harper shook her head.

Miranda's gut tightened. "What did he do?"

"He told me it was none of my business. 'Excuse me?' I said. 'I'm the charge nurse on this floor, so it's very much my business.'"

"He didn't like being questioned."

"No, he did not. He didn't answer me. He just stared at me like I was mud he'd just wiped off his shoe. And then he left the room and took the syringe with him. Most doctors have egos, but this one, it was like he thought he was God, Himself."

He had a god complex for sure. "What happened to the patient?"

"Well, I had no idea what Dr. Musgrove had given her. I had to assume it was something she needed. But then an hour later, the patient coded."

"Coded?"

"She stopped breathing. Fortunately another nurse was in the room at the time and noticed she was gasping for breath. We got Mrs. Ogden into ICU and discovered she'd had a morphine overdose. Another doctor administered naloxone in time. That's the antidote. It saved her life."

Miranda drew in a breath. "Good grief. Did you report what you saw?"

"I told another doctor about it. He said I must have been mistaken. It was that charisma, I tell you."

"He didn't want to blame Musgrove for it."

"No."

Miranda was feeling sick.

"The next patient wasn't so lucky."

"Oh?"

"Her name was Auclaire. She'd had surgery for a pinched nerve in her neck. She should have been fine. But two days after surgery, she was gone. One of the other nurses on the night shift said he saw Dr. Musgrove coming out of Mrs. Auclaire's room around one in the morning the night before."

"And did that nurse report Dr. Musgrove?"

Ms. Harper raised her palms. "He didn't see enough to prove anything."

"And the higher-ups would have taken Musgrove's side, right?"

She nodded. "Like I said, he had that charisma. I think he could make anyone believe anything. I tried not to think too much about it, but then there were three more patients who died on the floor. They were all Dr. Musgrove's. Finally, I couldn't stand it any more."

"What did you do?"

"I went to his office to talk to him. I asked him about all these patients we were losing. I asked him whether he put the overdose of morphine in Mrs. Ogden's IV. I was willing to give him the benefit of the doubt. Maybe he'd misread the chart. Maybe he'd made a miscalculation."

"What did he say to that?"

"He got really angry. 'How dare you question me?' he said. 'Are you an MD? How long have you studied neurosurgery?' He had these big dark eyes. He scared me."

That god complex. He'd have to believe he was invincible to keep killing his own patients. To think he had the right to decide who lived and who died. "What did you say to him?"

She wagged her finger in the air. "I told him this had to stop or I'd talk to the Chief of Medicine next."

Like her mother had at Suburban General. "And did you?"

"Never got the chance. Sorry. I need something a little stronger." Ms. Harper got up, went to a cabinet along the wall, and took out a bottle that looked like vodka. She poured a fingerful into her lemonade and took a swallow.

Then she came back to her chair and fixed Miranda with a look so intense, she thought the poor woman might burst into tears. "The next day, I came into work and went into the breakroom. Someone had left a plate of cinnamon rolls out on the table. They looked good, and I hadn't had breakfast, so I ate one."

Miranda held her breath. She knew what was coming next.

"About twenty minutes later, I started having sharp pains in my stomach. And then it got worse. I ran for the ladies room, made it into a stall, and got rid of everything I'd eaten for a month. That's what it felt like, at least. I swear, I never barfed like that before in my life. Still can't stand the thought of cinnamon."

She eyed her drink, then set it down again. Apparently, the taste of vodka wasn't much better right now.

"Anyway, when it stopped and my head cleared, I realized someone else was in the next stall, doing the same thing. It was Gracie, another nurse I worked with. She had eaten two of those rolls. She was really sick and had to be taken to the emergency room."

Miranda's blood was starting to boil again.

"Somehow, I had the presence of mind to rush back to the break room. There were still two cinnamon rolls sitting on the table. I grabbed them. My first instinct was to toss them in the trash, but then I thought, no. This is evidence. I wrapped the whole plate up in plastic wrap and took it straight to the police station."

Bold move. "And what did they do?"

"They were skeptical. It was hard to believe someone in the medical profession could do something like that. One officer told me I was hysterical. But finally they sent someone out to investigate. You must know the rest."

She did. "They tested the rolls and found arsenic."

Ms. Harper nodded. "And ant poison in Dr. Musgrove's desk. As you know, Musgrove was arrested, tried, and sentenced to five years."

"And now he's out."

"He sure is." Ms. Harper's eyes grew dark. "I started my blog the day he was released."

And started locking her doors, Miranda bet. "You asked people to contact you if they knew anything about Musgrove. Has anyone done that?"

She grimaced with disgust. "You."

"No one else?"

"The only person was Mary Auclaire."

"Mary Auclaire?"

"Mrs. Auclaire's daughter."

"The patient who died after surgery for a pinched nerve."

"Yes. Mary had done a lot of research on the doctor. She learned he grew up in Doncaster, Indiana."

"I know that."

Ms. Harper blinked at her in surprise. "How?"

Miranda sat up on the edge of her seat. "Ms. Harper. You have to know Musgrove poisoned you and the other nurses to shut you up."

"Of course, I know that."

"He did the same thing to my mother seventeen years ago when she reported him for overdosing his patients at a hospital in Oak Park, Illinois. He left a sponge on a set of stairs he knew she'd be using. She fell and broke her neck. I can't prove it, but I know he killed her."

Cora's hand shot to her mouth, and her eyes teared up with the compassion of a true medical professional. "Oh, my word, Ms. Steele. I'm so sorry."

Miranda appreciated the sympathy, but that wasn't her point. "Don't you see? I talked to a cleaning man who worked with my mother. He knows what Musgrove did to her. And Musgrove worked at a hospital in Cedar Rapids where personnel knew what Musgrove was doing to his patients. If we can get all the data together, and get people from three different hospitals to testify, we can build a solid case against him. We can put him away for good."

All at once, Ms. Harper's mouth opened, and her face brightened with hope for a moment. Then just as suddenly, it all disappeared, and she slumped back in her chair.

"I'm sorry, Ms. Steele, but that won't work."

"Why not?"

"When Musgrove got out, some of us pooled our money and hired a private investigator to find him. If he was working somewhere, we thought at least we could warn them."

"And?"

"The investigator looked high and low for him. Musgrove was nowhere to be found. He told us the surgeon must have left the country."

Miranda felt her heart stop. "Left the country?"

"That's what he said. Musgrove can't show himself here now. He probably can't get a job in the medical profession. Instead he's hiding somewhere overseas."

Miranda's head was whirling with denial. "But he's probably still killing people."

Ms. Harper shook her head. "I know, but there's nothing we can do. He'll never be found. He's gone for good."

CHAPTER THIRTY-TWO

Miranda drove around Kankakee, not knowing where she was going, feeling as sick as if she had eaten one of those poisoned cinnamon rolls herself. Her mind a blur, she drove through neighborhoods, under a rusty railroad bridge, alongside a river.

A horn blared at her, and she realized she had swerved into the wrong lane. She veered back and shook herself.

She was in no shape to drive. She had to pull over.

A few yards ahead of her was a church. She turned into the parking lot, took the center spot, and turned off the car.

Shaking all over, she put her hands over her face. She felt more lost and alone than she had in a long time. She was supposed to be a top PI, but she couldn't avenge her own mother's death. She couldn't put away her killer. She couldn't even find him.

Leaning her head back against the seat cushion, she stared out at the three tall stained-glass windows of the church. She could just imagine her mother up in Heaven, shaking a finger at her.

"I told you, Miranda. Life is no joke."

No, and neither was death.

"Oh, Mama. Why didn't you talk to me? Why didn't you warn me about Leon? Why didn't you tell me you faced him down?"

Her mother had stood up for her, when no one else had. If only she'd known that. If only she'd had some kind of relationship with her. But she was gone. The emptiness inside her was like a huge hollow cave. For a moment, she thought it might overwhelm her.

And then the tears came.

She sat there, bawling, wetting her hands and arms like a little child. She felt like a child. A child longing for its mother. Her mother had been so brave. After Miranda's father left, she'd fought through her despair and found a good job. She'd toughed it out, working her way up to become an RN. She'd stood up to Leon. She'd stood up to Musgrove. Just the way Miranda might have.

And then it hit her.

They *were* alike. Just like Alice Whitaker and Hardwick Yontz had told her. Because she was like her mother, somehow Miranda had survived Leon. After Leon, she'd learned to fend for herself. And after she joined the Parker Agency, she'd fought her way to become a private investigator. And she'd found she could muster up the courage to face killers like her mother had. Because she carried her mother's genes in her.

She knew that now.

And for the first time in her life, she could truly mourn her mother's death. And the loss of her.

She sat there, crying for a long time.

And then she pulled herself together, found some tissues, and dried her face and eyes and hands. She'd find a way to locate Musgrove. She'd go to the ends of the earth if she had to.

And she'd make him pay for what he'd done.

But how?

Before she could come up with an idea, her cell rang.

It was Becker.

Daring to hope for the impossible, she grabbed the phone. "Tell me you've got something."

"Oh. Hi, Steele. Well, I've got the kids fed and settled down with their homework."

Miranda closed her eyes in frustration. "So you're just getting started?"

"No. The install for Fontana Construction crashed. There was a driver incompatibility, wouldn't you know. I'll fix it later. So I had a chance to look over the stuff you sent me and do some digging."

Her hopes rising, she sat up. "And?"

"And did you know Musgrove was arrested in Peoria nine years ago? He was working at a place called Hilltop Community Hospital, and he poisoned some of the nurses there with cinnamon rolls laced with arsenic."

"Yes, I know that."

"You do?"

"Found it out when I googled him like you told me to."

"Oh. Do you know how he got the job at Hilltop?"

That she hadn't figured out. "No."

"When he applied for the job, he faked recommendation letters from medical centers in Florida. He also claimed to be board certified. He wasn't, but nobody bothered to check. They needed the help too badly."

"How did you find all this out?"

"Don't ask."

"Okay." She wouldn't.

"So you know he grew up in Doncaster, Indiana, right?"

"Right." From the articles she'd sent him.

"I did some digging around in the town records."

How Becker got into those, she'd never guess. She was glad he was one of the good guys.

"Musgrove was an only child. His mother died in a car wreck when he was fifteen."

She didn't know that, either.

"I sent you part of an article."

She hadn't even heard it come through. She swiped to her messages and read the quote from the local paper with the headline, "Tragedy in Doncaster."

Local police report that at about nine p.m. yesterday, a vehicle was driving east on the main highway. A westbound semi was in the wrong lane, heading straight for the vehicle. The driver blew his horn, but the semi didn't respond. Panicking, the driver of the vehicle swerved off the road, barreled across several yards of grass, and crashed into a tree. The driver survived, but the passenger was killed.

"The passenger was Musgrove's mother?"

"Yeah, pretty horrible."

"Gosh. That had to cause some trauma."

"It did for his father. He eventually became a cocaine addict and had to be institutionalized."

Wow. So Daddy wasn't there to make all the problems go away. Fifteen. The year before the incident with the quarterback on the football field. That was why Musgrove had been such a bully.

He had anger issues.

And when he lost his father's support, Musgrove must have channeled his rage into studying medicine. But he couldn't keep it bottled up. He took it out on his patients and started killing them because he couldn't deal with his loss. It was a theory anyway.

But it didn't tell her where Musgrove was.

"Steele? You still there?"

She drew in a breath. "Yeah. Thanks for the great work, Becker. As usual, you're amazing. But the problem is, we can't locate him."

So she was back to where she'd been before the phone call.

"Wait, Steele. I'm not done."

There was more? "Okay."

"I really had to cut some corners for this, but I found out after he got out of prison, Musgrove changed his name."

What? Of course, he did. "No wonder nobody can find him."

"He changed it to John Musk. I've been looking for hospitals where he might have worked, but haven't found anything yet."

Was knowing Musgrove's new alias enough? It still could take years to find him. How many would die during that time? She felt sick again.

"I found something else."

"What?"

"There's a John Musk living in Doncaster."

Miranda stared at the phone. She couldn't believe what Becker had just said. "You mean he changed his name and went back home?"

"That's what it sounds like."

Or John Musk was an old neighbor whose identity Musgrove had stolen. "Are there any hospitals in the area?"

"Not sure. I'm looking into that now."

"Do you have an address for John Musk?"

"Yeah. Right here."

"Text it to me."

"Sure thing. What are you going to do, Steele?"

She punched the location into her phone. That town in Indiana was only about three hours away. With this baby, she could get there in less. With some luck, and some help from the authorities, she could have Musgrove in custody by tonight.

"I'm going to Doncaster."

"Oh?"

She started the car, and the Tesla came to life. "Great job digging this up. Oh, and Becker?"

"Yeah?"

"You're a good friend."

"You, too, Steele. Be careful."

"I will." Her hopes rising again, she hung up and pulled out of the parking lot as fast as she could.

CHAPTER THIRTY-THREE

It was midafternoon, but there was still a slight chill in the air of central Kentucky.

Parker plodded through the woods, the smell of poplar trees in his nose, the baying of the hounds in his ears, his new footwear pinching his toes.

After he'd called in Santana's abandoned vehicle to the authorities, he'd checked into the first motel he could find for a three-hour nap. When he awoke, he'd indulged in a stack of local pancakes and scrambled eggs, and then headed to the nearest clothing store.

The best he could find was a camouflage T-shirt, matching twill pants, a mesh duck hunter's cap, and a pair of mountain hiking boots that needed breaking in.

He'd given the torn suit he'd worn for two days to the shop owner for disposal.

And then he'd joined the local police as they canvassed the area around the vehicle, going house-to-house through the small nearby towns, and farm-to-farm in the surrounding acres. Officers in Bardstown had done the same with similar results.

Some had seen his picture on the news, but no one had seen anyone matching Santana's description in person.

Frustrated, Parker had joined the officers in the woods.

The hounds had picked up Santana's scent from the abandoned vehicle, and it was logical to assume Santana had kept to the forest to avoid being out in the open. The vegetation they were moving through might have kept the scent intact, though experts disagreed on how long that would be.

Looking grim, Special Agent Lawrence Rymer from the FBI trudged alongside Parker, a few yards away. "I have to say the timing is not in our favor, Mr. Parker."

An obvious understatement.

"If we were tracking the suspect shortly after he abandoned that Cutlass, we could limit the radius of the search area. But after more than a month—"

"I know. It's nearly impossible."

"I wouldn't say nearly. I'd say it's hopeless."

Parker didn't see much difference in the words. And yet they had to try. They had to keep going. "According to my informant, Santana had a specific destination in mind."

"But he never reached it."

"That we know of." Though he wasn't in any of the homes Parker and the police had visited there so far.

"Still, we can search only so much land. If the suspect is outside that range, I'm afraid we'll be out of luck."

Special Agent Rymer was definitely not an optimist. But Parker was finding it difficult to muster any confidence himself.

Suddenly, the hound's baying began to escalate.

Parker picked up his pace. "Have they found something?"

"Let's find out."

Alongside the agent, Parker raced toward the sound, his gut tightening. Over dead twigs, around fallen branches, through the weeds and foliage they ran.

At last, they heard the voices of the other agents and officers who had gone on ahead of them.

Rushing toward the direction of the sound, Parker slipped a hand into his pocket, where he'd tucked the second Glock he'd borrowed from police within the last twenty-four hours. If the authorities found Santana here in the woods, he wouldn't be able to use it. He'd have to settle for watching him being taken into custody, and perhaps the pleasure of testifying against him at trial.

He would not throw away his own life by walking up and shooting the vermin.

Unless there was a legitimate reason to.

"There they are." Rymer pointed up ahead to a hill where several men stood holding back the dogs.

Parker raced up the incline to the spot and peered between two of the officers.

In a small clearing was a circle of rocks cluttered with charred wood.

"A campsite," Parker said to the group. "Was he here?"

"Titan seems to think so," said the man holding the hound whose nose was digging through the dead leaves near the fire.

Parker bent down and carefully laid a hand against one of the logs. It wasn't warm, but it was recent.

Rymer followed suit. "He's been here within the last hour, I'd say."

Parker's chest rumbled. "Where is he now?"

The dog at the far end of the site suddenly took off. "Do you smell him, boy?" said the officer who'd just let him go.

"After him." Parker rose and shot across the patch of ground and into the trees where the dog and officer had just disappeared.

He raced through the poplars and oaks and pines, barely aware the forest floor beneath his feet was rising in elevation. He left Rymer behind, passed the group of officers who had been at the campsite, and had almost caught up to the hound when the forest became less dense, and the land opened up to a wide rushing river.

On the bank stood a man.

His hair was long and dark, and he had on a drab gray shirt and baggy pants of the same color. Not a suit. He had something dark in his hand.

Was it him?

Parker was taking no chances. He drew the Glock from his pocket and aimed at the center of the man's back.

"Don't move."

"What?" the man said.

"Drop your weapon."

"Weapon?"

"What you're holding."

The man did as ordered.

"Put your hands up."

Slowly, the man raised his arms. Then he cussed into the air. "I told Willie I'd pay him for his truck. No need to set the law on me."

"Turn around," Parker barked.

The man obeyed, and Parker's heart sank down to the earth.

It wasn't Santana. It was a young man, probably twenty years his junior.

One of the hounds broke into the clearing and bounded toward what the man had dropped on the ground. He put his nose in it, sniffing furiously.

"Good boy." The officer in charge of the dog leashed it and pulled it off the thing.

Another officer picked it up with a gloved hand.

"What is it?" Parker asked.

As the man turned over the object in his hands, Parker recognized it. Black, leather, about a size twelve.

"It's a man's dress shoe, sir."

"Not any dress shoe. A Louis Vuitton. Santana's brand."

CHAPTER THIRTY-FOUR

The young man danced from foot to foot. "Oh, man. Oh, man."

"Where did you get this?" Parker growled.

"At my campsite. A couple miles back that away." He gestured toward the woods in the direction they had come from.

"And what do you know about it?"

"Know about it? Nothing."

"What are you doing in the woods alone?" Parker demanded.

He shook his shoulders. "I had a fight with Donelle last night. She's my girlfriend. She said I was fooling around on her. Me. Can you believe that?"

At this point, Parker might believe anything.

"Anyway, I was so mad, I got into my truck and drove into the woods."

In the truck he owed Willie for, Parker surmised.

"I went to the spot where I usually park when I go hunting. I slept in the bed. I carry a sleeping bag back there. When I woke up, I was still mad, so I went for a walk in the woods to cool off."

"A rather long walk."

"Like I said, I was really mad. Anyway, after a while I calmed down and realized I was freezing, so I sat down and built me a fire. I sat there for a good long while thinking about Donelle. She's really special. I really love her, you know?"

One of the officers cleared his throat. "What does that have to do with that dress shoe, son?"

"After a while, I got thirsty. I mean really thirsty. And hungry. I knew about this river and thought I could get me a drink and maybe a trout. But I didn't have my gear with me. So I looked around for something to carry water in, and I found that shoe."

Parker narrowed an eye at the boy. "No man who went with the shoe?"

"No. There wasn't a soul around, I swear. I found that shoe under a tree root. Looked like it had been there awhile."

The shoe did appear quite worn. It was caked with mud and had probably been rained on several times.

"Are you sure you saw no one else around here?" said the officer holding the shoe.

"No one, sir. Can I put my hands down now? My arms are getting tired."

"At ease," said the officer in charge. "We'll take you back to your truck now. And we'll need to see your license and registration."

The young man rubbed his arms. "Am I in trouble?"

"Not at the moment."

The officers couldn't hold the young man. He'd done nothing wrong.

"That's a relief." As they started back through the forest, he gave them a toothy grin. "I need to get home and get cleaned up. I've made up my mind. I'm going to ask Donelle to marry me."

CHAPTER THIRTY-FIVE

As Parker followed Rymer back to the spot where Santana's vehicle sat, a sense of emptiness settled upon him.

But now Rymer became the optimistic one. "We'll test the shoe for DNA, of course, but by Titan's reaction to the scent, I'm convinced it belonged to Santana."

"I agree, but that still leaves us with too many unanswered questions." Yet again.

"The condition of the shoe tells us it was left there at least a week ago."

"Or longer." It was cracked and stained and worthy of the trash bin. That was no consolation. "In three weeks time, Santana could have made his way out of Kentucky, possibly out of the country."

"Or he could still be somewhere in these woods." Rymer scanned the trees surrounding them. "On the other hand—"

"Say it."

"He could be dead."

The idea didn't set well with Parker's revenge fantasy. But he had to admit it was a possibility.

Rymer extended a hand. "If Santana's body is in these woods somewhere, those hounds will find him. We'll start again in the morning."

"I'll see you then."

As Rymer walked away, Parker stared at the bumper of Santana's brown Cutlass still peeking over the crest of the hill.

It had turned out the vehicle had not had a mechanical breakdown.

It had run out of gas. Santana and Phineas must have pushed it over that hill in an attempt to hide it. Their plan had nearly worked.

There were men in the nearby trees, watching to see if Santana would return with a can of gas after laying low for several weeks.

Parker doubted he would. The Cutlass would eventually be taken into the station for processing, which would yield no information that they didn't already know.

With a burning sense of failure, Parker stared off into the woods. Was he out there?

His own hunches had gotten him only so far. Why did he think he could pursue the likes of Santana on his own? He needed help. He needed someone with more finely tuned instincts than his own.

He needed Miranda.

CHAPTER THIRTY-SIX

The sun in his eyes, Parker drove back to the roadside motel he'd slept in. As soon as he arrived, he checked out and headed to Louisville. There he checked into an upscale inn with a courtyard.

Something Miranda would like, though she might not admit it.

He'd find a chic Szechuan restaurant where he could indulge her wildest spice fantasies. The culinary sort. The physical sort would come later.

He sat down on the edge of the bed to make sure it was comfortable. It met his expectations. He would need a new suit, he decided.

He pulled his phone from his pocket and imagined Miranda in his arms again as he searched for the next available flight from Atlanta. He could almost smell her scent, sense the feel of her skin against his.

Then he stopped scrolling.

He checked his log. There had been no missed messages from her while he'd been in the woods. She hadn't even tried to contact him. She was angrier with him than she had been in a long time.

He didn't blame her.

It might take him a while to convince her to get on a plane and join him here. He'd wait to book the flight.

Hesitating, he turned the phone over in his hands. If only he hadn't kept his search for Santana from her. If only he hadn't gone off to Florida without her.

Filled with genuine contrition, he dialed her number.

The phone rang four times.

His stomach tightened. Was she ignoring his call?

Finally the ringing stopped. It was replaced by the sound of rushing wind. She was in her car.

"Miranda?"

Static crackled in his ears. "Parker?"

He'd get straight to the point. "My darling, I want to apologize."

She let out a short bitter laugh. "Apologize? You mean for going off to Florida to hunt for Santana without me?"

He winced. Her sharp words cut deep. "That's precisely what I mean."

"Did you find him?"

"No. In fact, that's why I'm calling. I need your help."

No reply. For a moment Parker wondered if the call had dropped. "Miranda? Are you still there?"

He could hear her inhale before she answered. It wasn't enough. Not yet.

And then she spoke in a clipped business-like tone. "Sorry, Parker. I don't have time to chase Santana. I'm going after the doctor who killed my mother."

Parker shot to his feet. "What?" Her mother had died seventeen years ago. She fell down a set of stairs.

"His name's Musgrove. Dr. Bogart Elrod Musgrove. Served a five-year sentence for poisoning some nurses. Changed his name to John Musk. Lives in a town called Doncaster. Becker can give you the details."

Details. Becker. "Where are you?"

"Just crossed the Indiana state line. I should be in Doncaster in just over two hours. I rented a Tesla. It zooms. Gotta go."

She hung up.

Dumbfounded, Parker stared at his phone. His face flushed with anger. He'd call her right back and demand she get on a plane to Louisville.

Who was he kidding?

He tossed his phone onto the bed. What in the world was she doing? Going after a doctor who'd poisoned nurses? A doctor she thought had killed her mother? She was doing it again. Running straight into the hands of some dangerous psychopath.

In a Tesla. A vehicle that could reach two hundred miles an hour.

He picked up the phone again and looked up Doncaster, Indiana. It was almost three hours away.

Well, two could rent a Tesla. There had to be one available in this town.

He would find it. He only hoped he could get to her and stop her before it was too late.

Stuffing the phone back in his pocket, he rushed out the door as fast as he could go.

CHAPTER THIRTY-SEVEN

Miranda sniffed and swiped at her nose as she blinked back hot tears. She couldn't cry now. She was driving eighty miles an hour.

How dare Parker call and apologize like it was that easy? Didn't he realize how much it hurt for him to cut her out of his plans? How useless it made her feel?

And now he wanted her help? Now he wanted her to join him? It made her so mad, she wanted to scream. But she couldn't think about it now, or she might run off the road.

She had to get to Doncaster. She had to find John Musk.

Daring to press the accelerator a little more, she flew over the flat landscape, past cows and horses and sheep, and acres of Midwestern corn.

It was almost dusk when she reached the outskirts of Doncaster.

She rolled into town, past a gas station and the Dollar Store, and onto a narrow street of small but well-cared-for homes that had been built close to the road. A sidewalk ran on either side of the street. Elm trees shaded the nicely kept yards.

The address Becker had given her for John Musk was at the far end. She drove down to it, pulled up to the curb, and turned off the car.

It was even smaller than the other houses. A square single-story with a brick exterior. No garage. No car parked near it.

Was he home?

She had to check. If he was, what was she going to say to him? Anything but that she was a PI, she decided, getting out of the Tesla.

She made her way up the walk to the stone steps and the front door and rang the bell.

Nothing.

One of the bricks in the steps was missing. She could say she was selling insurance. "Do you know how much that could cost you if somebody tripped on that and sued you?"

She could at least get his name out of him.

She rang again and listened. No animal sound. No footsteps. Was he at work? She shuddered to think what that might mean.

Turning, she noticed the sound of a motor cutting through the air. She went down the steps, across the lawn, and peeped around the corner of the house.

A neighbor was on a riding lawn mower, cutting the grass. He spun around and started on the patch alongside his house, coming her way.

"Hi there," she called.

No answer.

Miranda waved an arm. "Excuse me, sir."

The man was chubby, maybe in his early fifties. He wore a striped shirt, a Colts cap, and a grin on his face. Must like mowing grass.

Miranda waved both arms. "Hey!"

No response.

This guy had to know something about John Musk. She had to talk to him.

She stepped onto his lawn and into his path, her arms out in front of her.

"Stop!" she yelled, like a traffic cop.

The man looked up, saw Miranda, and gaped at her.

He stopped the mower about two feet in front of her, and the noise died down.

"What in tarnation are you doing there, Missy?" He pulled two earbuds out from under his cap. "I might have run you over."

She was quicker than that.

"Sorry to bother you, sir, but I'm wondering about your neighbor." Miranda waved an arm toward the other house.

The man got off the mower, took off his cap, retrieved a handkerchief from his back pocket and wiped his face.

"My neighbor? Why are you asking about him?"

"Where is he?"

"Where is he? How should I know?"

"Uh, cause he's your neighbor?"

"I mind my own business."

"Do you know his name?"

"Why?"

She was going to have to go down the detective route. She pulled out a card and handed it to him. "My name's Miranda Steele. I'm a private investigator, and I'm looking into a matter he might be involved in."

The neighbor's eyes went wide as he glared at the card. "Is John in trouble?"

"That's his name? John?"

He nodded. "John Musk."

Miranda's stomach twitched. She was close. "What do you know about him?"

"Not much. He's not here a lot. When he is, he's pretty self absorbed. We don't talk much."

"Do you know where he works?"

He thought a moment. "No, but I assume he's a doctor."

"Why?"

"Because like I said, he's not here much. And when I do see him getting out of his car, he's always wearing scrubs and a white coat."

It was Musgrove. And he was at it again. How many had he killed this time? Once more, Miranda felt nauseated.

She pulled her phone out of her pocket and scrolled to the picture of Musgrove she'd snagged from Cora Harper's blog. "Is this what he looks like?"

The neighbor squinted at it. "Hard to tell. It's kinda small."

Miranda moved to the still she had taken from one of the videos. "How about this? Is that him?"

"John was on trial? What did he do?"

"Where is he now?"

"He hasn't been home for days. I have no idea."

This guy couldn't tell her much more. She'd try another angle. "Is there a hospital around here?"

The neighbor nodded. "County General. It's a twenty-minute drive straight down Highway 231."

"Thanks. I appreciate your help." She was already heading back to her car.

"Wait. What do I do if he comes back?"

"Give me a call right away. And lock your doors."

CHAPTER THIRTY-EIGHT

"What do you mean, he's not in your database?"

Miranda stood at a sleek onyx counter inside County General Hospital, dealing with yet another stodgy, rule-following HR person.

This one was tall and slender and young. She looked more like a fashion model than an office worker, and she reminded Miranda a little of Sybil at the Agency. Her title was Specialist.

She regarded Miranda with a lofty air. "I mean we don't have a John Musk on our payroll."

"Are you sure? He's a neurosurgeon."

The woman glanced down at the business card Miranda had given her. "Of course, I'm sure, Ms. Steele. There's no one named John Musk in Neurosurgery or in any other department."

"Try Bogart Musgrove, then. Dr. Bogart Elrod Musgrove."

With a glare, the Specialist let out a huff of annoyance, but she complied and tapped at her keyboard with long golden nails that had to be fake.

She paused.

"Well?"

The specialist shook her head. "I'm sorry, Ms. Steele. We don't have anyone by that name, either."

This was maddening.

Miranda yanked out her phone and showed the woman the still from Musgrove's trial. "Is there anyone on your staff who looks like this guy?"

The young woman's nose wrinkled as she looked at the screen. "Why is that man in a courtroom?"

"He poisoned several nurses in a hospital in Peoria. He served five years for it."

"We wouldn't hire someone like that."

"Not knowingly. But he may have faked his records. And like I said, he changed his name to John Musk."

"And like I said, Ms. Steele, there's no John Musk on our payroll."

Dismissing her, the woman picked up her phone and began to dial.

No point in asking whether they had their employees's photos on file. Or if they had facial recognition software they could run them through.

Miranda jabbed a finger toward her card. "Call me if you learn anything."

The woman nodded, nearly rolling her eyes.

Disgusted, Miranda turned on her heel and headed out the door. She was done with hospitals.

She was going to the police.

CHAPTER THIRTY-NINE

She drove back into town and found the police station housed in a small metal building on a wide open field with a water tower in the distance. The smell of cow was in the air when she got out of the Tesla and marched to the front door.

Inside she found a plain-looking waiting area. Along the far wall stood a plain-looking counter. Behind the counter were two plain-looking officers in dark uniforms and buzzcuts, who were guarded by a see-through barrier shield.

The one standing at a set of shelves filing papers was on the chunky side and looked to be in his early thirties. The one in a chair poking at a laptop seemed to be in his mid-twenties and had a beanpole physique that reminded her of Holloway.

Miranda walked up to the counter and spoke into the metal mouthpiece. "Excuse me, officers, I need some help."

The older one strolled over to the counter and grinned at her. "Hello, ma'am. Welcome to Doncaster."

Raising a brow, Miranda eyed the name tag under his badge. "How do you know I'm from out of town, Officer Tobin?"

Tobin chuckled. "First off, you're dressed like a city slicker."

"City slicker?" Miranda hadn't heard that term since she was a kid.

"No offense, ma'am. What I meant to say is that I know everybody who lives here."

Nice dodge. But also good news. "Do you know a John Musk?"

Tobin frowned and scratched his head. "Can't say that I do."

Not such good news.

The younger officer in the chair chuckled.

Tobin cleared his throat and turned serious. "What's this about, ma'am?"

Reaching into her pocket she dug out another business card and slid it under the shield. "My name is Miranda Steele and I'm a private investigator." Then she took out her phone and held up Musgrove's trial photo. "I'm looking for this man. He goes by the name of John Musk. His real name is Bogart Elrod Musgrove. He's a doctor. A neurosurgeon."

Tobin took a look at the photo. "Is he wanted for something?"

"He was convicted of poisoning nurses in Peoria seven years ago. He's been out of prison for two years. I have reason to believe he killed several patients in three different hospitals by overdosing them."

Drawing in a breath, Tobin gave her the cop eye. "Do you have any proof of that?"

Miranda thought about the HR woman in Cedar Rapids who hoped Musgrove was in jail. She thought about her mother who had reported Musgrove at Suburban General. She thought about Cora Harper, who had confronted Musgrove and gotten poisoned for it. Would their testimony be enough to put him away?

Probably not.

"I will if I can talk to him." She wasn't going to let that sanctimonious surgeon intimidate her. She was going to get a confession out of him.

Tobin rubbed his chin. "If I were you, I'd go over to County General and talk to somebody there."

"I already have."

He seemed surprised at that answer. "And?"

"And he's not there."

"Well, there you go." Tobin turned back to his filing.

How could he be so dismissive? "Look, I've got an address for Musk. I dropped by earlier and talked to his neighbor. He recognized Musk from that photo."

Tobin looked over at the officer at the laptop as if to ask for his opinion.

He only shrugged.

Miranda was getting frustrated. "Do you have any other hospitals around here?"

Tobin chuckled again. "There's Midwest."

Why was that funny?

The other officer sat up. "That place is haunted."

"Midwest was shut down over a decade ago," Tobin explained. "It's abandoned."

A taller officer emerged from the back and headed for the coffee machine along the far wall. "What are you talking about Midwest for?"

Tobin nodded toward Miranda. "This lady says she's looking for a doctor she thinks killed some people, Webster. But nobody at County General knows him."

The officer named Webster filled his cup and took a sip. "Hmm. There was another lady in here a few days ago talking about a doctor. Said she thought he killed her mother."

Miranda started. "What was her name?"

"Let me think. Mary? Yes, that was it."

"Mary Auclaire?"

He snapped his fingers and pointed at her. "That was it. She thought she could find that doctor at Midwest. I told her no way."

"How can you be so sure?"

Tobin chuckled again. "There's nothing there. The place is falling down. It should have been condemned a long time ago."

"That's what I tried to tell her," said the officer with the coffee cup. "But she said she was going to check it out anyway."

Check it out? What did that mean? What did Mary Auclaire know about Musgrove? "Where is she now?"

He shrugged. "Must not have found what she was looking for and moved on."

"Where is this Midwest place?"

Tobin gave her a wary look. "About five miles northeast of here, near Rocky Creek."

"Okay." Miranda started to look it up on her phone.

"You won't find it on the GPS. Besides, it's locked up tight. You can't get in there, and neither could Ms. Auclaire."

"We'll see about that. And I'll find the place."

"Wait. If you're that determined, Ms. Steele, let me draw you a map." Tobin reached for a sheet of paper, sketched out a few lines on it, and handed it to her. "Here you go. Good luck, ma'am."

She had a feeling she'd need it.

Miranda took the paper and folded it. "Thanks for your help," she muttered, and left the station as fast as she could.

CHAPTER FORTY

Miranda stopped at the Dollar Tree and picked up a flashlight, some batteries, a box cutter, a screwdriver, a box of paperclips, and a nifty pouch to carry it all in that hooked onto her belt.

If she had to break into that abandoned hospital, she was ready. Except that she wished she had her Beretta with her.

The sun had set while she was in the police station, and the Tesla's headlights streamed over the asphalt like panthers on the prowl as she headed to her destination. Following Tobin's map, she left the main highway and rumbled over dirt roads and narrow paths until she came to a sharp curve.

Was it a driveway or another road?

Ancient looking oaks grew on either side of an unpaved trail, and from what she could see, they would soon become a dense forest.

But this was what the map indicated, so she turned onto it.

For a while, she saw nothing in front of her but darkness and dirt. And then she reached a wrought iron gate. Both sides of it were rusted and hung open on old stone posts.

An unsettling welcome, but at least it told her there was something ahead.

She drove through the opening, steering the Tesla over the bumpy ground. Here the tree trunks were thicker and the leaves of gnarled branches overhead brushed the top of her car. As she drove, her skin began to tingle and itch.

The ants.

Not the physical kind. The psychological ones. The ones she was all too familiar with. She shivered with the sensation. Did it mean she was close? Did it mean she was about to find Musgrove?

As if in answer, suddenly the forest opened to a clear area. A large yard.

And there it was.

The gigantic building that was Midwest Hospital.

Or at least, she hoped so.

Leaving her lights on, she got out of the car and used her flashlight to make her way through the weeds to get a better look.

The air was chilly. Wind rustled through the leaves, like the sound of ghosts. Though it was dark, under the shadows of tall elms, she could just make out the outline of a huge red brick structure. A building that could rival some of the biggest mansions in Buckhead. But it was more than a house. It was an institution. A section on the far side of the place had collapsed, but the rest was still intact. More or less.

Ivy covered most of the front. A rotting second story porch of the entrance sagged in the middle. The columns supporting it looked like they might give at any minute. She could see why Tobin and his buddies thought she was nuts. This building was uninhabitable. Why did Mary Auclaire think she'd find Musgrove here?

There was an engraving over the tall entranceway.

Miranda lifted her flashlight to read it. "Midwest Hospital.' This was the place all right. Then she took a few steps to the left to see the rest of the sign that was hidden behind ivy leaves. And the full name.

Her stomach clenched.

"Midwest Hospital for the Insane."

Officer Tobin hadn't told her that part.

Squinted at the sign, she peered through the vines and saw a tiny red light. Was that a security camera? Did it mean someone was inside watching her? Maybe the place wasn't so uninhabitable.

The ants started to bite.

Not going in that way, she decided.

She stepped back and got her bearings. Maybe the right wing of this edifice was in better shape.

She headed for the far corner where the bricks made a ninety-degree angle.

Wishing she'd brought a machete, Miranda fought her way through the bushes and weeds growing around the yard. Then the foliage cleared and a dirt footpath appeared.

She ran her flashlight to the end of it, and once more, her heart nearly stopped.

A white Toyota Corolla sat beyond the weeds.

She rushed over to it and yanked at the handle. Unlocked. Nobody inside. But she could smell the faint scent of perfume. She crawled behind the steering wheel and over the driver's seat to the glove compartment.

She opened it and riffled through papers.

It was a rental. At the bottom of the agreement was the client's signature in a neat, legible handwriting.

"Mary Auclaire."

She was here. But where? The taller officer said she'd come into the station a couple days ago. Had she found Musgrove here?

Miranda's gaze ran up the side of the building. Her breath caught. There was smoke coming from a chimney. And there was a light in a room on the third floor.

Police.

Maybe this was enough proof for them. She dug in her pocket for her cell and dialed. Or tried to dial.

No signal.

She couldn't wait for the police to get here, anyway.

She stuck her phone back in her pocket and swept her flashlight over the building. It landed on a set of steps leading to a side door. Bingo.

She hurried over to it and turned the handle. It was open.

Locked up tight, huh? Then she thought of the camera she'd spotted. Was this a trap?

Hesitating, her heart pumping adrenaline through every fiber of her being, she pondered her options.

They were slim.

But Musgrove was her mother's age. Around sixty now. From the photos she'd seen of him he was pretty emaciated. She was in good shape and trained in martial arts. She could handle him.

And if Mary Auclaire was somewhere in this insane asylum, there was no time to lose.

Again she wished she had her Beretta with her. Instead she dug in her Dollar Store pouch and pulled out her new box cutter. She slid the blade open and reached for the handle.

With a vague wish that Parker was at her side, Miranda flung the door open and stepped inside.

CHAPTER FORTY-ONE

Forcing down his mounting sense of dread, Parker raced over the miles of interstate as fast as he dared.

The Tesla Roadster he had rented in Louisville was speedy, but not fast enough.

Where was she?

He'd called Dave Becker the moment he was on the road and had learned it all. Now he couldn't stop thinking about what Dave had told him about the man Miranda was after.

He was the doctor who had signed the death certificate for Miranda's mother. He was suspected of overdosing several patients with morphine and killing them. No one could prove it, but the man had been convicted of poisoning nurses with arsenic in Peoria. He had forged documents to get his job there and had not been seen since his release from prison. He had changed his name to John Musk and had likely gone back to his hometown.

Parker tapped the display on the dash and dialed Dave's number for the second time.

He answered right away. "Yes, sir. I'm still working on it."

"Have you found anything at all?"

"There's only one hospital in the area, Mr. Parker. County General. I've combed through their records, and there's no John Musk or Bogart Elrod Musgrove working for them."

"How many years have you gone back?"

"I started with the date Musgrove was released from prison."

The only information they had was that address for John Musk. Perhaps he had retired or was working in some other field. Once more, Parker's mind raced with the horrifying details Becker had supplied. The man was a monster.

"Actually, sir, there's one other place outside Doncaster."

"Oh? What is it?"

"It's called Midwest for short."

"What's its full name?"

"Midwest Hospital for the Insane."

Dear Lord. Still, a fitting place for a killer to be employed. "Have you looked into their records?"

"It was shut down a little over ten years ago."

His jaw tightening, Parker considered the news. "You said Musgrove's father was a cocaine addict and had to be institutionalized. Could he have been sent to Midwest?"

"I don't know, but I can try to find out."

It would be a reason for Musgrove to return home, depending on his relationship with his father. Nonetheless, it was a thread to follow.

"Keep digging," he told Becker. "I've just passed Franklin. I'm less than an hour away."

And he hung up and pushed the Tesla harder.

CHAPTER FORTY-TWO

The air was stagnant and smelled of rot. Sparse light from a ceiling bulb cast eerie shadows over ash-gray cinder brick walls.

Holding her box cutter in one hand, her flashlight in the other, Miranda inched down the long musty corridor she'd found herself in when she entered the hospital. Glancing up, she took in the gnarled pipes running the length of the ceiling.

This place was like something out of a horror movie.

Stepping around the debris scattered on the floor, she passed a set of rusted bed rails leaning against the wall and a broken wheelchair that was missing its back. Supplies. This had been a hospital, after all.

Correction. A hospital for the insane. An asylum. Down here she might come across all sorts of equipment once used to treat the mentally ill, some of it in probably not very humane ways.

As she skirted around a stack of dusty crates, she didn't want to think about what might be in them.

The passageway seemed endless. She felt as if she were trapped in some hidden underworld that would go on forever. She needed to find a way up to that lighted room she'd seen outside, but she didn't see a set of stairs anywhere.

She was reconsidering the front entrance when she spotted a square metal door on the wall.

Utility panel?

There had to be a power source somewhere, but was this it? The thing was pretty rusted and the ceiling above it was decayed. Definitely not up to code. Would it even do any good to try to cut the power?

As she pondered the option, a loud thud came from somewhere down the hall.

Miranda jumped, nearly dropping her flashlight.

Instincts kicked in and she spun toward the sound, holding out the box cutter, her chest pounding.

She waited.

Boom. There it was again. Boom. Boom.

What in the world was that?

She held up her light and spotted a recess in the wall. Hurrying over to it, she found a door.

It looked like it belonged in a prison. Was this where they used to put patients they couldn't control?

As she stared at the thing, she heard another boom.

The steel of the door shuddered.

Miranda's breath caught and her throat went dry. Someone was behind that door, trying to get out.

She put her box cutter in her pouch and tried the handle.

Locked.

Then she noticed a small panel was fastened to the door at eye-height. It had a cover over it. Miranda grabbed its handle and shoved it open.

Standing on tiptoe, she peeked inside.

Behind the door was a good size room, maybe ten-by-ten with walls of the same ash-gray cinder block as the corridor. No furniture. No benches along the walls. A single harsh light bulb hung from the ceiling.

And under the light stood a woman.

She seemed to be Miranda's age. Her stringy dark blond hair was matted to her head by a strip of cloth somebody had used to gag her.

A pair of nice pumps were on her feet. Her wrinkled skirt looked like part of a modest business suit. But the rest of her was covered in canvas. Her arms were wrapped around her inside sleeves that were fastened behind her back.

Someone had put her in a straitjacket.

Immobilized, she'd been throwing herself against the door in a futile attempt to escape.

Panting through her nose, she stared at Miranda with terror in her eyes.

She had to be the renter of the Corolla outside.

"Are you Mary Auclaire?" Miranda whispered through the jail cell opening.

Her eyes went even wider with shock.

Furiously she nodded and grunted something Miranda couldn't understand. She guessed it was some version of "Help!"

"My name is Miranda Steele. I'm a private investigator. I've been looking for a man named Dr. Bogart Elrod Musgrove."

The woman grunted some more.

"Is he here?"

Mary Auclaire nodded and raised her gaze to the ceiling.

Fear shot through Miranda's body. That bastard was upstairs.

"Hold on. I'm going to get you out of here."

She stepped back and studied the door.

That lock would be hard to pick with the paperclips she had. Two thick hinges held the door in place along the opposite side. When she was in construction, she used to be pretty good at taking off doors.

Digging into her pouch, she pulled out the screwdriver and went to work on the top hinge.

She reached up, wedged its tip under the cap of the pin, and pulled down on the handle. It would have been nice to have a hammer, but she could make due with her weight and a little leverage.

After some yanking and maneuvering, the top pin came out. A little more work, using her foot this time, and the bottom one was out as well.

Now what?

"Hey, Mary," Miranda whispered as loudly as she dared. "Give this door another shove."

There was silence for a moment, and then came the sound of footsteps and the now familiar boom.

The door shuddered and tumbled forward.

She couldn't let it crash, or they'd be discovered for sure.

Miranda swung her arms and caught the heavy thing just before it hit the floor. After getting a better grip, she managed to lay it on its side without too much noise.

It still blocked part of the opening.

Mary stood on the other side looking helpless.

She had to get her out of that jacket.

Gingerly Miranda climbed over the bottom of the door and stepped into the cell. It smelled worse than the corridor.

The poor woman looked miserable.

"Let's get that gag off." Miranda turned her around and studied the knot at the back of her head.

It was tight. She'd have to use the box cutter. She got it out and went to work. "Hold still. I don't want to cut you."

"Mmm," Mary replied.

Miranda slipped her hand under the cloth and spread her fingers. Carefully, she began stroking downward, as if she were brushing the woman's hair, though it was the material she wanted. It was thick and tightly woven. Her blade cut through only a little bit of it at a time, and she had to be patient.

Not her strong suit.

But she kept stroking and cutting and finally, the fabric gave way.

She pulled off the gag and tossed it to the floor.

The woman spat out the rest of the gag, then turned to Miranda. "Thank you. Thank you so much." She looked like she was about to cry.

"You're welcome, but we're not done here. I have to get you out of this jacket."

Miranda turned her around again and examined the back. It was a maze of buckles and straps. The ends were tied into more tight knots. Again, cutting would be faster than trying to untie them. She picked a strap and began to work on it.

"That man upstairs killed my mother," Mary whispered.

"I know."

"How? And how did you know my name?"

"Hold still now."

"I'm trying."

The fabric of the straps was even thicker than the gag. And the thing was pulled so tight, Miranda wondered how Mary could even breathe. She had to be careful not to cut into her flesh with the razor blade.

"I went to see Cora Harper in Kankakee. She told me what happened to your mother. She said you visited her, and that you were hunting for Musgrove."

"That's how you found me?"

"Not exactly. I went to the police. They told me about this place and that you had stopped by the station on your way here."

"I wanted them to help me find Dr. Musgrove, but they didn't believe me."

"They didn't believe me, either. How did you know Musgrove was here?"

"It was a hunch. After I went to see Cora Harper, I found a surgeon who had worked with Dr. Musgrove in Peoria. He said one night they were working late, and Dr. Musgrove opened up to him. He told him about growing up in Doncaster and that his mother had died in a car accident when he was just fifteen."

"Yes, I know about that, too."

"How did you know?"

"From some research somebody did for me." No need to go into details about Becker and the Parker Agency.

"I started to look into the local papers here. I found several articles about Musgrove's father."

The same ones Becker had dug up, she'd bet.

The first strap came free. Now for the others. Miranda continued cutting while Mary told her more.

"The senior Musgrove took his wife's death hard."

"I can imagine." Miranda twisted the stubborn material and made another slice with her blade.

"So hard, he began to self medicate. Eventually he became a cocaine addict. He got so bad, one night he walked outside naked with a butcher knife and attacked a woman he'd never seen before on the street. He killed her."

"Killed her?" Miranda had to stop cutting. At the moment, she didn't feel steady enough. "He's as insane as his son."

"Exactly. He was declared unfit for trial and was institutionalized in this hospital. Dr. Musgrove visited him regularly here. It seems they were close."

What a lovely family.

One more strap to go. Shaking off her shock over the news of yet another murder, she attacked the material with renewed vigor. "But why would Musgrove be here now? This place was closed over a decade ago."

"Yes, but the elder Musgrove died here. There's a cemetery on the property. He's buried there. That's why I thought Dr. Musgrove would come back here."

"Good guess."

"What I found was that he was living in those upstairs rooms. And still killing people. There's a body up there."

Dear Lord. Finally, the last strap came loose.

Miranda didn't have time to ask Mary for more details. She helped the woman out of the jacket, pulling it over her head.

As she came free, Mary shook herself and put her hands to her face. "I don't know how I can thank you. I don't know what he would have done to me if you hadn't found me."

"I'm glad I did."

Mary looked down at her feet. "My gun."

"Gun?"

"I had a conceal-and-carry in my ankle holster. He took it."

She was bold to bring a weapon with her, but that meant Musgrove was armed. If he knew how to shoot. Miranda's guess was that most surgeons wouldn't have time to learn.

No time to worry about it.

She turned to Mary. "Right now, you have to get out of here. Get in your car and get to the police station as fast as you can." She rolled up the jacket and handed it to her. "Take this with you. Tell Officer Tobin we've got their proof."

She climbed back over the door and helped Mary into the corridor. "There's an exit that way. It's not too far. Your car's a few feet from it."

"Okay. What are you going to do?"

Miranda turned toward the dark passage. It had to lead upstairs at some point. "I'm going to get a confession."

"From Dr. Musgrove?"

Miranda nodded. "That sonofabitch killed my mother, too."

CHAPTER FORTY-THREE

At the very end of the corridor, at last Miranda found a staircase.

It was hidden behind a door. The door stood open. Not a good sign, but it wasn't stopping her.

Up she went.

The steep dusty steps curved around the wall, and Miranda could only hope the old wood wouldn't cave in. Or creak too loudly. They seemed to go on forever, but at last she reached the landing to the second floor without incident and ascended to the third floor.

There she found an old pale green door with the same peeling paint as the rotting walls.

This one was closed.

No way to peek inside before she opened it. For all she knew, Musgrove could be standing on the other side waiting for her with another straitjacket. Or Mary Auclaire's gun.

She'd take her chances.

Flipping off the flashlight, she tucked it into her pouch, took out her box cutter, and once more extended the blade. It was probably dull by now, but she couldn't take time to change it. If she could hit a vulnerable spot, she could still incapacitate him.

Steadying her nerves, she held out the blade and pushed the door open.

No one here.

Instead, she stood at the end of another long passageway that disappeared into darkness. compared to the dungeon she'd left downstairs, this one was a tad cheerier. If you could use that word for this place.

The walls were covered with a dingy yellowed paint. An ugly brownish stripe ran down the middle, dividing the top from the bottom. Artistic. Except for the surfaces that, like the ones below, were peeling like skin after a bad sunburn.

The floor was relatively free of debris.

He'd cleared it out, she thought, her nerves tingling.
He had to be here. She had to find him.
If she didn't before the cops got here, he'd run away. He had to have a vehicle somewhere on the property. He'd drive off and disappear into the ether.
No. She wasn't going to let that happen.
Before her stood a myriad of doors. He had to be hiding behind one of them.
She picked one and opened it.
An empty room. No one in here.
But what was this place? There was an odd smell In the air.
Stepping inside, she found an old table stretched along another dingy wall. It was littered with stands of test tubes filled with liquids. Next to the tubes sat a large microscope. Beyond that stood a beaker on an unlit Bunsen burner with something in it that was a sickening green color.
Was this some kind of makeshift lab?
On the wall was a whiteboard covered with notes she couldn't decipher. Formulas? Chemistry symbols?
In the far corner stood a worn desk. She moved over to it.
Handwritten notes were scattered next to an old computer that didn't look like it was connected to the internet. Musgrove had a doctor's handwriting. She couldn't read anything. What did he think he was working on?
Beyond the desk the room took a ninety-degree turn, becoming L-shaped.
She dared to step around the corner and immediately inhaled an animal scent.
Then she saw the cages.
A row of them sat atop a shelving unit stuffed with bottles of chemicals. Inside the cages, white mice were hooked up to tubing attached to small bottles filled with liquids.
Was that the concoctions he'd been cooking up in the beakers and test tubes? Some of the mice were lying dead on the floor of their cages. Others were barely moving.
What was that all about? Had Musgrove settled for killing mice because he couldn't get to any humans in a hospital?
Bewildered by the sight, she moved on and found another door beyond the cages.
This one had a frosted pane, so once again she couldn't tell what was behind it.
Her box cutter extended, she barged through.

CHAPTER FORTY-FOUR

Now she found herself in a large open space with a high ceiling. Several tall arched windows stretched across the far wall.

All of them were boarded up.

No one was in here, either, and everything was completely silent. But the air had a chill in it, and the odor here was even more nauseating.

No, not completely silent. There was a very faint dripping sound.

Then Miranda realized the space had been set up like an operating room. Across the room, large round lamps stood on poles around a table. They were dark now. On the table lay a body covered with a white sheet.

The body Mary Auclaire had told her about.

Feeling sick, Miranda moved toward it, taking in the scene. Three plastic bags hung from IV poles. They seemed to be sending fluids into the body through tubes. Or maybe it was out of the body. A red liquid moved in one of the tubes. Was it blood?

Still, the set up looked a lot like those mice in those cages. Except for the large pan under the bed. It seemed to be there to catch liquid dripping from the body. That was the sound she'd heard.

Her skin crawling, Miranda bent over the corpse. The face was uncovered. It was a woman. She was young.

Miranda raised her hand and dared to touch her cheek. She was cold, of course. But colder than a normal dead person. She was frozen.

Was she thawing?

Who was this victim?

Miranda didn't know, but she was going to make Musgrove pay for what he'd done to her as well as to all the others.

Turning away, she spotted another door in a corner.

That's where that sonofabitch had to be hiding.

As quietly as she could, she hurried across the floor and shoved open the door.

It was a kitchen. Empty.

The overhead light was bright as day in here, but there were still no windows.

Against the wall stood an old retro stove and fridge in an ugly avocado color. Cabinets that badly needed refinishing completed the look. In the middle of the room sat a dinette set with a formica top table.

And on the table was a plate of cinnamon rolls.

Miranda sucked in a breath. Did he really think she'd fall for that?

Then she heard a floorboard behind her creak.

It was him.

CHAPTER FORTY-FIVE

Turning her head, from the corner of her eye she could see pale blue scrubs and a white lab coat, like the neighbor had described. She recognized the dark hair, the bony features and dark sunken eyes she'd seen in the pictures of him.

She spun around, sweeping her box cutter in the air as she did.

But he was ready.

He grabbed her by the wrist and twisted. "What are you doing in my house?" he growled.

Yow. He was stronger than she'd thought.

"I came for you, Musgrove." Widening her stance, she twisted the other way and almost broke his hold, but he grabbed her with his other hand, trapping her.

"I know who you are."

"And I know who you are. A killer." She pushed up, trying to get at his face with the blade.

He ducked and swerved.

She yanked her arm toward him as hard as she could and managed to nick him on the ear.

It didn't even faze him. His grip tightened.

She kicked out at his shins.

Quickly he stepped to the side, and she missed.

His reflexes were good, and his grip on her arm was getting even tighter. If she could spread her fingers, she could get out of his hold, but she would drop the cutter. Instead, she hacked at him like a drunken landscaper trimming hedges, her blade going back and forth in the air as they arm wrestled.

The dude could fight. Must have learned how in prison.

Taking a risk, she turned in to him and lifted her leg. If she could get a knee kick to the side of his leg, she could take him down.

But now he caught her off balance. He grabbed her other arm, spun around with her, and slammed her against the wall.

The box cutter clattered to the floor, taking Miranda's heart with it.

He kicked the tool away and glared at her, his foul breath beating against her face. "You aren't going to stop me. No one can stop me."

"Think again, you creep." She struggled against his grip, tried to kick again, but he was too close to her.

And then he did something strange. He let go of one of her arms.

She grabbed a wad of his hair and tried to yank it out, but he didn't seem to even feel it. She tried to pull him down, but she couldn't budge him.

And then she saw him take something out of his pocket.

Burlap.

A strange scent filled the air.

Her heart pounding, she bent over, getting ready for a hard headbutt to his solar plexus.

Mistake.

He moved faster.

It was a burlap bag he'd had in his pocket, and now he slipped it over her head just as she lunged. She panicked, lashing out with her fists and feet, but it was like punching at a giant marshmallow.

Where were her skills? Her reflexes? She should have spent more time in the gym lately.

She struggled hard, but the bag on her head was soaked with a liquid. She couldn't help breathing it in. Now she recognized the citrusy chemical smell. Chloroform. Of course, he'd have a stock of that back in his lab.

She tried holding her breath, as she fought with him, kicking out at his legs and missing. She swung for his face and hit only air. She tried again and must have gotten him in the face, because he let out a groan.

But the blow did no good.

She was getting woozy. Everything was starting to spin. She had to get this thing off her head. She reached for her own neck, tried to get her fingers under the burlap, but he was holding it tight around her throat. She couldn't hold her breath any longer. She opened her mouth and inhaled.

Her knees turned to jelly, and she slumped to the floor.

She kept throwing punches, but none of them landed. She couldn't even tell where he was now. The whole world was getting dark.

And the last thing she heard was the echoey sound of Musgrove laughing with satisfaction.

Once more, he'd won.

CHAPTER FORTY-SIX

The little town of Doncaster would have been a charming country spot, if it hadn't been the home of a doctor who'd become a maniacal killer.

Nearing panic, Parker pulled into the police station parking lot and fairly leapt out of the Tesla. He hurried inside and found a middle-aged officer reading a document behind a see-through barrier at the counter.

"Pardon me, Officer. I don't mean to sound like an alarmist, but we have a situation on our hands."

Frowning, the man looked up at him. "A situation? What kind of a situation?"

"My wife has been looking for a physician who's suspected of murder. I have a Doncaster address where he resides under an assumed name. I believe my wife is at his home now. I'm on my way there, and I need a police escort."

The officer scowled at him in silence.

"The physician goes by the name of John Musk. His father suffered from mental illness. He was institutionalized here."

The officer raised a brow and reached for a business card. "Is your wife Miranda Steele?"

"Yes."

"She was in here earlier tonight. She said she'd already been to Musk's house. If the institution you're talking about is Midwest Hospital, that's where she went."

Dread pounded in Parker's temples. "I need to find her right away. I fear she might be in danger if that man is there."

The officer scoffed. "He's not there. Midwest isn't livable. It was closed down a decade ago."

Parker forced down his anger. "I know that, Officer Tobin," he said, reading the man's name tag. "But my wife is very persistent. I'm revising my request for a police escort to Midwest Hospital, then."

Officer Tobin scratched his head. "We're pretty short-handed right now."

Another officer appeared from the back with a coffee cup in his hand. "Are you talking about Midwest again?"

Tobin nodded toward Parker. "Third person to inquire about it."

"Third?" Parker wanted to shake the man.

"There was another woman in here asking about the place a few days ago."

"Two women express concerns over a murderer who's somewhere in your town and you do nothing?" Parker was ready to threaten to sue.

"Now, look here, Mr.—"

"Parker."

"Mr. Parker. Neither of those ladies had anything but suspicions. Not even probable cause. We can't drop what we're doing and go looking for someone without any evidence."

Parker leaned over the counter. "If anything has happened to my wife, I will hold you and your department personally responsible."

"Mr. Parker—"

Before he could finish, the door to the station slammed open, and a woman rushed in.

Disheveled and wild eyed, she ran to the counter. "Officer Tobin, we need your help."

"Ms. Auclaire, what are you doing back here?" said the officer with the cup. "Did you find something at Midwest?"

"I found Dr. Musgrove. He's got a dead body in one of the upper rooms. And he put me in this."

She shoved a bundle of canvas onto the counter.

Officer Tobin eyed the bundle with alarm. "Is that what I think it is?"

"It's a straitjacket," Parker said with revulsion. His heart breaking, he turned to the woman. "Ms. Auclaire, did you see my wife at Midwest? Her name is Miranda Steele."

"Yes," she nodded. "She got inside and rescued me. She told me to come here and get help."

"Where is she now?"

"She went after Dr. Musgrove."

Panic engulfed him. It was his worst fear. "Then there's no time to lose."

Finally, Tobin and the other officer started to move. "We'll get a couple of squad cars out there right away."

That would take too long. And Parker still had the Glock he'd borrowed from the local authorities in Kentucky in his pocket.

He turned to the disheveled woman. "Can you take me to Midwest, Ms. Auclaire?"

Her eyes still wild, she nodded. "Yes."

"Let's go."

Without waiting for permission or advice from the officers, Parker rushed out of the door with her.

But as he helped her into the Tesla and ran to the driver's side, he had a sinking feeling they were already too late.

CHAPTER FORTY-SEVEN

She was floating again.

Up and down. Up and down. She must be on a boat. Or maybe a raft in the middle of the ocean.

It was cold. Shivering, she reached for a blanket.

She couldn't move.

With a start, Miranda opened her eyes. But her vision was cloudy, and she couldn't see much at first. She blinked a few times and a ceiling came into view. High. Dingy. Cobwebs in the corners. Then she remembered.

Midwest Hospital.

She tried to lift her head. It felt like an anvil. Or rather, like it had been hit with an anvil.

She recalled the bag that bastard Musgrove had pulled over her. How could she have let him get the best of her like that? But it didn't seem like she'd been out long. Twenty to thirty minutes for chloroform, she remembered from her training. Depending on how much she'd inhaled.

Surely he couldn't have meant for her to wake up this soon. But here she was. Must have been all that coffee she drank today.

Again she tried to raise her head.

It fell back onto the pillow. Ugh. Wait. Pillow? Was she in a bed?

There was a mattress under her. A blanket over her. Managing to turn her head this time, she saw a rail next to her. She was in a hospital bed.

She looked down. Under the blanket she was in a hospital gown. Where were her clothes?

She looked up and saw a pole next to the bed. There was a bag hanging from it. And a tube running from it—and into her arm.

In horror she stared down at the needle taped to her arm.

That bastard had hooked her up to an IV.

She had to get that needle out of her.

Panicking, she tried to move her hands. She couldn't.

Finally she managed to raise her head high enough to see that her wrists were bound to the rails with plastic zip ties.

Terror rippled through her. Her heart pounded. She couldn't breathe. She couldn't think. She wanted to scream at the top of her lungs, but she didn't dare.

"Get hold of yourself," she whispered through gritted teeth. "You can handle this."

Sure, she could. She'd gotten out of restraints before.

Forcing air into her lungs, she took in three deep breaths and felt herself calm a bit. Her head cleared a little more.

Then she began working on her right wrist. She twisted it one way, then the other. It didn't work. She needed leverage. She needed some force.

Make it small. She pressed her fingers together as tightly as she could and pulled.

The tie was too narrow. She couldn't get her hand through it.

What was she going to do?

"You're awake."

Miranda choked back a cry as Musgrove came through the door.

She could see the whole room now. It was smaller than the kitchen or the large space where she'd found that body. It must have been a patient's room once upon a time.

Musgrove stood in the doorway in his scrubs and white coat studying her as if she were one of those mice in his lab. She stared back at him, taking in his dark features, his wavy dark hair parted down the middle, his receding chin and thin lips, the savage look in his dark sunken eyes.

But it was what was in his hand that made Miranda quake inside.

He was holding a hypodermic needle.

Keep your cool. Get him to talk. Mary Auclaire would be here with the police soon. She hoped. If she could get a confession out of him, they could book him for murder tonight.

Putting on a fierce expression she glared at the man. "I know who you are, Musgrove. I know everything you've done."

"Do you, now?" Chuckling, he locked the door behind him, put the key in his pocket, and took a step toward her.

"You won't get away with it."

He scowled. "You have no idea what you're talking about."

"I know exactly what I'm talking about."

He wagged a finger at her. "I know who you are, too. I heard you downstairs with that other intruder."

Just as she'd feared, he had a surveillance system down there.

Miranda raised her head as high as she could. "Her name is Mary Auclaire. You killed her mother in Hilltop Community Hospital twelve years ago."

He didn't answer. Instead he narrowed his dark eyes at her. "When I heard you say your name, it sounded familiar. And then after a moment or two, I remembered *her*. Hilda Steele."

He needed a moment to recall plotting her mother's death? "That's right. Hilda Steele was my mother. She worked at Suburban General Hospital in Oak Park, Illinois. She reported you for killing patients there. Like you did later at Cedar River and Hilltop."

He let out a grunt of disgust and moved to a small metal table at the side of the room. He set the hypodermic needle down on it and began removing things from his pockets. Rubber gloves. What looked like alcohol wipes. Small bottles with liquid in them.

Nerves spiked in Miranda's stomach. She had to get loose. While he had his back turned, she worked on the zip tie that was farthest away from him.

But she still had to get that confession.

"After you were released from prison for poisoning nurses in Peoria, no one would hire you, right? So you came here to Midwest to keep on killing. Is that woman in the other room your first victim here? Or are there more?"

He turned and glared at her with loathing in his eyes. "Why would I do that? This is a dreadful place. My father was confined here for more years than I can bear to think of. Conditions here were beyond horrific. My father was experimented on. He suffered horribly. After ten years, he managed to throw himself out of one of the upper story windows."

She remembered Becker had told her the senior Musgrove had committed suicide. She hadn't known the details.

"They buried him out in the yard. I was too late to save him."

What did that mean?

She watched him pull the seal off one of the bottles, open one of the wipes, and use it to clean its top. Nice of him to care about germs.

Maybe if she probed deeper she'd hit a nerve and get him to confess. "You lost your mother, too."

Now he turned to her with loathing in his eyes. "You are not allowed to speak of my mother."

Suddenly Miranda realized all of Musgrove's victims she knew about were female. Why hadn't she thought of that before? "Was your mother abusive? Did you hate her? Did she make you hate all women? Is that why you started killing them?"

"How dare you make such accusations? I loved my mother. I worshipped her. She was the finest woman who ever lived. She was a saint."

Really? "And then she went and died on you."

He let out a cry and spun around. He leaned over the bed, wagging the needle in her face. "You are so like your mother. You understand nothing. You don't even know how my mother died."

But she did know. "It was in a car accident. There was a semi going the wrong way down the highway, heading for your mother's car."

"You don't know the rest."

Yes, she did. "Your father swerved to avoid a head on collision. But he overcorrected and hit a tree. Your mother was in the passenger seat. She died on impact. Your father couldn't stand the guilt. That was why he ended up in here."

Letting out a cry of anguish, he shook his head. There were tears in his eyes. "Why am I surrounded by imbeciles? You understand nothing." He turned back to the table and began to slip on his gloves.

She sat up as best she could, still working on the zip tie. "Wasn't that how it went?"

"It was the summer before my junior year in high school."

"You were fifteen."

"I had just gotten my learners permit. I was so excited about driving. I begged my mother to let me take her to the grocery store for practice." His voice quivered as he spoke, and he stared down at the table, trying to control his emotions.

Miranda's mouth dropped open as she realized what he was trying to say. "*You* were the driver?"

"My mother told me to slow down, but I wouldn't listen to her. And then suddenly that semi came out of nowhere. I tried to avoid it. Then all at once, the road was gone and we were bouncing over the shoulder and then onto grass. I lost control. I panicked. And then we hit. I can still hear the sound when we crashed into that oak tree. I can still feel the impact. It crumpled the front of the car like an accordion. And then I saw my poor sweet mother slumped over in her seat. Blood oozed from her forehead. I wanted to do something to save her, but I was too late. The police came and pulled us out of the car. I was in shock. For a long time, I thought I'd never get over it."

No wonder he was so unhinged. She almost felt sorry for him. "You were just a kid."

"My father said he'd never forgive me. Not unless I found a way to bring her back. And so I promised him I would."

Bring her back? What in the world was he talking about?

He seemed calmer now. He took the cap off the hypodermic needle and stuck it into one of the bottles. Then he slowly pulled the plunger back to withdraw the liquid.

Miranda felt her pulse quicken. "That's morphine, right?"

His lip turned up in a smile. "I thought you knew all about me."

He was going to kill her with that stuff like he had all the others.

"By some miracle, my mother's cells were not badly damaged. Thankfully the cryonics procedures at the time were good, and we got her taken care of in time."

Cryonics? Was he saying what she thought he was saying? "What's that got to do with overdosing patients with morphine?"

"Don't you understand? I did it so that they can live. I knew if I could just perfect my methodology and get the dosages right, I could do it. I could bring them back."

"Bring them back?"

He reached for the second bottle on the table and drew more of that stuff into the syringe. "I wasn't able to finish my experiments. Someone always got in my way. I got close with Mrs. Auclaire, but they came and took her body away before I could finish."

Miranda's skin began to crawl.

"That was why I came here to Midwest. I had more testing to do before I had the answer. I had to finish my experiments on vermin. Not the ideal circumstances, but it was the only way I could save her."

Was he saying what she thought he was saying? "Save who?"

"My mother, of course."

"But your mother's dead."

"She was preserved. I told you we had her taken to a cryopreservation laboratory."

"You mean you had her—frozen?"

He held the syringe up, tapped a finger against it. "You saw her for yourself, didn't you? In the operating room."

That woman on the table in that big room was—his mother? Miranda recalled the body-sized pan catching water under her bed.

She was thawing.

Dear Lord. He thought he was saving people by killing them? He actually believed he could bring them back from the dead? He did have a god complex. This man was totally, completely insane.

She had to get away from him.

He removed the needle and put it on the table. Then he screwed the syringe into a port on the IV line and began to squeeze the plunger. "It will take about five minutes for the first dose."

"Hey, I'm already alive, so you don't have to bring me back." Of course, so were all of his victims.

He grinned. "No, *you* I want dead."

Miranda's breath grew shallow with terror. Her mouth went dry. Her heart pounded in her head.

And then she got mad.

He must have sensed her outrage. "You should be grateful, you know. I have the drugs to make you suffer terribly before you die, if I wanted to. But I'm a compassionate man. This way you'll simply relax, fall asleep, and slip into eternity without even knowing it."

What a sweet guy. Her chest began to heave. She could only hope her anger would stave off the effects of the drug. "The police are coming for you, Musgrove. They're going to catch you in the act. You'll get the death penalty."

He ignored her. "When I finish with you, Mother will be ready to wake up. I can't wait to speak to her again. When I was a boy, we used to spend a lot of time in the kitchen. She taught me how to bake cinnamon rolls. I made a plate for her for when she wakes up."

The rolls on that table in the kitchen. They must not be laced with arsenic.

She couldn't think about that now. The liquid in the syringe was going down. She felt herself getting woozy.

She had to do something. Now.

Suddenly she discovered her legs were free. Time to use them.

With what seemed like a gargantuan effort as fast as she could, Miranda raised her knees to her chin and kicked out at him with everything she had.

Her feet landed square in Musgrove's chest.

He tumbled backward, taking the IV pole with him, both of them clattering to the floor.

The stretched tubing jerked at the needle in Miranda's arm, and she let out a cry. Gritting her teeth in pain, she brought a knee up against the zip tie she'd been working on, and with three strong kicks, her wrist came free. She drew blood, but she couldn't think about that now.

She rolled over, yanked off the tape, and gingerly pulled the needle out of her arm. Yow.

Now both her arm and wrist were bleeding. It didn't stop her from getting the second zip tie open.

Her hand came loose just as Musgrove was getting up. "What do you think you're doing?" he shrieked.

"Stopping you, like my mother tried to."

"And she failed."

Ignoring his words, she pulled off her blanket and climbed over the side rail in her hospital gown. Her bare feet hit the cold floor sending a chill through her. She was weak and woozy from the morphine, but she managed to swoop down and pick up the IV pole.

She ripped the IV bag off it and tossed it in the corner. It spewed saline onto the floor and landed on a small nightstand in the corner she hadn't seen before.

Then she picked up the pole and used it like a baseball bat on Musgrove.

He was just getting to his feet as she swung with all her might. The pole got him in the stomach, knocking him down onto the floor again.

Taking a step toward him, she raised the pole and swung it the other way, smacking him in the head. This time she drew blood.

She still needed that confession. "Say it, you bastard. Say you killed my mother."

His demon eyes glowered at her.

The floor was slippery with saline. She wished she had her shoes on so she could stomp on his ankle. The IV pole was getting heavy in her hands. Her stance felt unsteady. The morphine must be going to work.

Not good.

Before she could get in another lick, Musgrove grabbed the end of the pole and used it to pull himself up.

She tried to get a wider grip on the pole, but as she did, he wrested it out of her grasp and pulled himself up by the bedrail.

While his hands were busy, she lunged and threw the best punch she could at his face.

He let out a cry as his neck twisted around with the force.

But she couldn't get him down. And now she was too close to him.

Recovering fast, he tossed down the IV pole and grabbed the tube that was on the floor. It was still leaking fluid.

She tried to turn and move away from him, but her feet were sliding.

In one swift move he swung the tubing over her head and around her neck.

She spun all the way around with her back to him and got one hand under the tube before it went tight.

Still, it was hard to breathe. She was feeling more light headed by the minute.

He held her tight against his chest and hissed in her ear, quivering with hate. "Your mother. She was so demanding, so fastidious, so stubborn. I warned her not to go to Administration. She refused to listen. I had to get rid of her."

Miranda twisted her hand under the tube and managed to draw in a breath. "So you put a sponge on the step in the stairwell you knew she'd take when she delivered medications."

He laughed. "The sponge was an afterthought."

"Afterthought?"

"I grabbed the sponge when I was in the operating room earlier that night. I had it in my pocket. I tossed it on the stairs to make her fall look like an accident. It was plausible. Everyone believed it."

What was he saying? "She didn't slip on that sponge?"

"Of course not. That was too risky a plan. I followed her into the stairwell and pushed her down those stairs. I heard her neck break on the way to the bottom. It was very satisfying."

She got her confession. The truth about what happened to her mother. He'd pushed her. It was a vicious premeditated act. And now she was going to pay him back for it.

Miranda began to quake with a rage she'd never felt in her life. It must have given her an adrenaline boost. She kicked out behind her and got Musgrove's inner thigh.

With a yowl, he let go of the IV tube.

She lunged forward and hurried to the door. It was locked. He had the key in his pocket. Crap.

Then she glared back at him in time to see him twist around and head for the corner. Where that nightstand was. What did he want in there?

He threw open a drawer and pulled something out, and pointed it at her.

Oh, my God, no.

It was Mary Auclaire's conceal-and-carry.

"You're not going anywhere, Miranda Steele," he screamed. "I tried to make this easy for you, but you refused to appreciate my humanity."

He raised the gun.

Miranda dove for the end of the bed.

Musgrove fired.

His bullet hit the wall, making a large crack in the plaster. He was as bad a shot as she'd thought, but this room was small. He'd get her sooner or later.

Unless he ran out of bullets.

"Go ahead and kill me," she cried. "You're still going to pay for everyone you killed. Especially my mother."

"I don't think so." He fired again.

This time the bullet hit the wall behind her. That was too close. Two rounds spent. She had no idea how many the weapon held. Five? Six? He'd get her before they were gone.

Suddenly on the outside of the door she heard footsteps and shouting. Was she hallucinating from the drugs?

No. Musgrove heard it, too. Aiming the gun, he turned toward the noise.

There was heavy pounding on the door. Then, with a loud crash, someone kicked it in and slammed into the room.

Parker.

He had a weapon in his hand.

Musgrove pointed Mary's gun at him and fired.

Miranda heard herself scream.

But Parker got his shot off first.

Musgrove's bullet missed and hit the far wall, bringing down a piece of plaster. But Parker's aim was perfect. It hit the monster right in the middle of his chest.

Musgrove stumbled backward, tripped over the IV pole, and crumbled to the floor.

Miranda recognized Officer Tobin as he rushed past Parker and bent over the body. "He's dead."

She couldn't believe it. She was shivering all over.

Smiling giddily at Parker, Miranda drank in the love she saw in his face.

It felt so good, she wanted to cry.

"Oh, Parker. You came to rescue me." Then she blinked at the camouflage duds he had on. "What in the world are you wearing?"

The room started to sway again. The morphine-and-adrenaline cocktail coursing through her veins was too much. She couldn't take any more.

Before she could hear Parker's answer, she slid to the floor and passed out.

CHAPTER FORTY-EIGHT

"Miranda!" The word seemed to bubble up from some underground pool. Miranda barely felt Parker's arms slipping under her and lifting her up. Mmm. Nice.

It seemed like a dream when he murmured against her cheek. "Oh, my darling. What did that monster do to you?"

His deep warm voice was real enough to make her smile.

There was an ambulance outside. And EMTs. Real medical people.

She heard them moving around, felt the gurney someone had put her on being hoisted into the vehicle, and sensed Parker climbing in beside her to hold her hand. That felt nice, too.

And then there was nothing.

When she opened her eyes again, she found herself in a hospital bed with an IV in her arm.

Fear pulsed through her.

"No. No." She rolled over and started to pull it out.

Someone grabbed her wrist. "Don't, Miranda."

Looking up, she saw Parker's handsome face. The best sight in the world.

Where had he come from?

"You're not at Midwest hospital anymore," he said in a calm, soothing voice. "You're at County General."

She squinted up at him, and he released her arm. "I am? What time is it?"

"Morning. Last night they gave you an antidote for the morphine and let you sleep off the rest. I should know, since I've been hounding the doctors for details about your condition all night."

Her gaze went to a chair in the corner with a blanket draped over it. "You slept here?"

"I wasn't going to let you out of my sight."

She could tell he was holding back the urge to scold her for going after a dangerous killer on her own.

She reached for his hand. "How did you ever find me in that awful place?"

He sat down on the bed and caressed her precious fingers. "I went straight to the police station when I got in town. I thought you had gone to John Musk's house and demanded a police escort there. Then Mary Auclaire burst in and told us you had rescued her at Midwest Hospital. She had a straitjacket in her arms."

"Yeah. That's what I found her in. I cut her out of it with a box cutter."

"A box cutter." There was admiration in his eyes.

"I told her to take the jacket to the police and get help. They believed her then, didn't they?"

"They did, but we didn't wait for them. Mary and I drove back to Midwest to find you. The police were faster than I had assumed and arrived just as we were going through the front door. Mary led us inside and upstairs. We found Musgrove's study. He had lit a fire in the fireplace. Then Mary showed us the dead body she'd found."

"That was Musgrove's mother. He told me his father had her frozen."

Parker was surprised. "Cryonics?"

She nodded. "He thought he'd found a way to bring her back to life. That was why he killed all those patients. He was using them as experiments. He was trying to bring them back before he used the procedure on his mother."

"Good Lord."

"None of his experiments worked."

"Of course, they didn't. A deceased body in a state of cryostasis has never been brought back to life. The cells are too deteriorated."

She didn't know how he knew that, but she knew he was right.

"The man was an egomaniac to think he could do such a thing."

"He had a god complex, alright." She rubbed her free arm, feeling creepy just thinking about it. "Guess what else Musgrove said?"

"Tell me."

"He told me he pushed my mother down that stairwell at Suburban General Hospital."

Now Parker's eyes were filled with indignation. "Your neighbor told us your mother slipped on a sponge one of the cleaning staff dropped on the steps."

Miranda sighed. "But I found out the hospital had done an investigation, and they made that cleaning person a scapegoat. It's a long story. Anyway, Musgrove said he threw the sponge on the stairs after he pushed her so everyone would think it was an accident. It worked."

"Until you started looking into it."

He must be really mad at her. Her shoulders slumped. "I'm sorry, Parker."

"For what?"

"For getting myself in trouble. Again."

As he had so many times before, Parker studied those lovely black lashes, the delicate angles of that strong determined face, those desperately blue eyes shining up at him, full of life.

Did she think he was angry with her? He had been.

But when he'd burst into that room last night and found, of all things, a doctor in a lab coat with a gun in his hand, he had feared the absolute worst. And when he had looked across the room and seen her standing next to the bed in a hospital gown, when he'd watched her crumple to the floor, he feared he had just seen her die before his very eyes.

When he'd rushed to her and found her pulse, he'd wanted to weep like a little child for joy.

Now all he felt was sheer gratitude.

He let out a slow breath and made his confession. "It was my fault. I shouldn't have gone to Florida without you. I should have told you what I was doing."

Did he mean that?

She looked into those intense gunmetal gray eyes and, as if it were possible, saw more love in them than she ever had before. This ordeal had shaken him as much as it had her.

Miranda shrugged. "I guessed what you were doing, anyway."

Tenderly he touched her cheek. "Nonetheless, if I had lost you because of that mistake, I couldn't live with myself. The truth is I can't bear the thought of being without you, Miranda. I love you with all my being."

His words were making her dizzier than that morphine. After all the horrors she'd been through, only Parker could make her so giddy with joy.

With a shaky laugh, she raised her fist and tapped him on the arm. "Right back at you, buster."

He smiled again, the sexy laugh lines around his eyes making her heart squeeze. "The doctors say you'll be fine. You have a strong constitution. How do you feel?"

She thought a moment. "Hungry."

His hearty laugh made her heart soar even higher. Guess he wasn't so mad, after all.

"I think I can remedy that. Let's see when we can get you released."

"Okay. But first." She crooked a finger at him.

Reading her thoughts, he leaned in and gave her a sensuous kiss that made her toes curl under the sheet. She had missed him so much.

Now this was living.

CHAPTER FORTY-NINE

After they got the doctor's okay, Parker insisted on dressing her. The police had found her clothes in a closet at Midwest, and Parker had retrieved her laptop and luggage from her rental, and had arranged for someone to pick up the car.

He insisted she wear the jeans and boots and T-shirt she'd packed.

"Does this have something to do with why you're dressed as an Army ranger?" She was beginning to like the look.

"Perhaps." He wasn't going to tell her until after she was fed.

Before they left, Officer Tobin stopped by and took her statement. He actually apologized for not believing her and said he was glad Parker was such a good shot.

When the nurse rolled Miranda out the exit in the wheelchair they insisted she use, she had to let out a squeal.

Along the curb sat a beautiful silver blue sports car. Its stylish lines and sleek design shimmered in the sun as if it were showing off its good looks.

"Wow," was all Miranda could manage.

Parker chuckled. "You're not the only one who can rent a Tesla."

"That's a Tesla? It's a lot cooler than the one I had."

"It's a second generation Roadster. A demo, actually. I had to pull a few strings with the rental company to get it." He opened the passenger door. "I'd like you to accompany me in this vehicle to Kentucky."

Kentucky? How had he ended up there?

"Or would you prefer to fly?"

He knew she couldn't resist. "I think I'd go anywhere with you in that."

As the nurse helped her to stand and Parker eased her onto the gorgeous buttery leather of the passenger seat, she whispered to him. "Are we going after Santana?"

"As I said on the phone, I need your help, Miranda. I've learned it's better if we work together."

Yeah, she'd learned that lesson, too. The hard way.

Mary Auclaire met them at the tiny local diner where Parker fed both of them French toast with strawberries and lots of strong black coffee.

After telling them for the hundredth time how grateful she was that Miranda had saved her life, Mary let them know she had called Cora Harper and related everything that happened at Midwest. The woman had been dumbfounded. But she promised she would write down everything and publish it in a new post on her blog as soon as possible.

Miranda would have liked to call her and tell her to keep her name out of her post, but she was too late.

While they were exiting the cafe, a gang of reporters accosted them with cameras and microphones.

A woman in a blue dress stuck one in Miranda's face. "How did you know Dr. Musgrove was a killer?"

"What brought the famous PI Miranda Steele to Doncaster? Did you know it was his hometown?" babbled a man behind her.

"How do you feel after surviving what he did to you?" said somebody else.

Where did these leeches come from? And how did they know so much? Some of them looked like they were from a TV station in Chicago.

The news of a serial killer traveled fast.

"I'm sorry, ladies and gentlemen," Parker told them in his smooth-but-stern tone as he eased Miranda away from the crowd. "We'll have to talk to you later."

Of which he had no intention.

Hurrying down the walkway, he helped Miranda into the Tesla, climbed in, and they zoomed off to the interstate.

CHAPTER FIFTY

Zipping along the highway in the sporty Tesla was exciting, but the Midwestern scenery was as flat as ever. Lots of farms, lots of fields, lots of cows, pigs, and horses, and a few trees.

After traveling about an hour, everything she'd been through in the last few days started to sink in, and Miranda realized she needed to call Aunt Lu. It took her a moment to get up the gumption, but finally she dialed the number and told her aunt she'd been right about her mother's death. There had been foul play.

At first, Aunt Lu started to gloat, but when Miranda explained who Musgrove was and everything he'd done, the woman was stunned.

"I guess you are a pretty good PI, after all," she said in her gruff Minnesota accent.

Miranda couldn't believe Aunt Lu would admit that. "I guess I am."

They talked a bit longer, and then Aunt Lu hung up with an invitation for Miranda and her handsome husband to come and visit her in Rochester any time they wanted.

Maybe they would sometime, Miranda thought as she put down the phone and stared out the window at the corn fields buzzing by.

Parker's low sensual voice roused her out of her thoughts.

"You haven't told me everything, have you?"

He could always see through her.

"No, I haven't."

"It might be good to talk about it."

He knew something was still bothering her—in addition to the aftermath of the ordeal she'd just been through.

How should she begin? Drawing in a breath, she started to spill. "When I was investigating Suburban General in Oak Park, I went to see the cleaning man they blamed for my mother's accident. His name is Hardwick Yontz."

"And?"

"And he knew who I was. He was friends with my mother, had worked with her for years. He called me 'Hilda's little girl.' Turns out she talked to him about me when I was a kid."

"Oh."

"When I started to ask him questions about her accident, he said I was like her. He said I came straight to the point, just like she did."

"Well, you usually do. An admirable quality, in my opinion."

He was trying to make her smile.

"And before that, I met a nurse at Suburban General. Her name is Alice Whitaker. She's a supervisor in the Neuro unit where my mother worked. Well, she's retired now."

"And she knew your mother, as well?"

Miranda nodded. "They were coworkers and friends, too. Close friends. She knew my name before I told her."

"My," was all Parker could say to that.

"She said I was direct like my mother, too."

"It's reasonable that you would have some of her characteristics. It doesn't follow that—"

"I'm not done."

Parker gave her a patient look of sympathy. He understood this was difficult for her.

Miranda glanced down at the high-tech dash. The GPS said they were halfway to their destination, and the landscape was just as monotonous. Plenty of time to talk. No way to avoid it now.

She drew in another fortifying breath. "Alice said she and my mother talked about their kids a lot when they worked together."

"Not uncommon."

"She told me my mother loved me very much."

Parker continued to listen silently.

"Alice told me she admitted to her she hadn't been a very good mother. She'd been devastated when my father left. And after I married Leon, somehow, she found out—what kind of a husband he was."

She felt Parker reach for her hand.

Her chest was heaving now. It was getting even harder to get the words out. But she had to. She wanted Parker to know.

"Alice said my mother told her she found Leon and told him if he ever hurt me again, she'd destroy him. She'd make sure he lost his job and went to jail."

Parker's grip on her hand grew tighter. She began to blubber. Baring her soul always embarrassed her.

The tears began to fall. They rolled off her cheeks and onto their clutched hands.

"Would you like me to pull over?"

She shook her head. She needed to keep moving.

She wiped her eyes with her hand. "Oh, Parker. I don't know how to process it all. I've always believed my mother hated me, that she saw me as a burden she resented. But now I know she really loved me. She stood up to Leon for me."

"I would say that's a good thing to know about."

"Yeah, it is. But I just feel so empty. I wish she would have talked to me when she was alive. I wish I could talk to her now. I have so much to say, and I can't. I don't even know how to think about her anymore."

"An emotional transformation like that doesn't happen in a day."

She sniffed and swiped at her nose. "No, I guess not."

Parker reached into his pocket and handed her his handkerchief. "But I would suggest you start by trying to forgive her."

He had had to do that with his own father.

She took the kerchief and wiped her face.

Parker grew quiet. They passed a few semis. A green interstate sign marking the next town came and went.

Then once more he gave her hand a squeeze. "I would say the best way to think about your mother is to believe she's looking down on you from up above, and that she's very pleased with you for solving her murder."

Now she did smile a little. Maybe that was the best way to handle it. But she had a feeling there would be several sessions with Dr. Wingate in her future.

And no doubt in Parker's, too.

CHAPTER FIFTY-ONE

After another hour and a half or so, they hit the Ohio River and crossed over into Kentucky. As they zoomed over the interstate and through the traffic around Louisville, Miranda's head began to nod.

When she came to, it was midafternoon, and they had been driving through woods for a while, following a road that veered this way and that around tall trees that were growing denser with every mile. Through their trunks, occasionally a low hill came into view.

When Parker turned off the highway and onto a curvy wooded road she sat up.

Now she was wide awake.

After another mile, Parker pulled the Tesla over to the side of the road and stopped.

Blinking in surprise, Miranda looked around. They were in the middle of a forest. "Where the heck are we, Parker?"

"The western side of the Appalachians."

"I figured as much. But what are we doing here?"

He turned off the car and studied her carefully. "Do you feel anything?"

She frowned at him. "Just that we've stopped moving."

He leaned closer to her. "Are your instincts telling you anything?"

Now she got what he was asking. "About Santana?"

"Yes."

She knew what he meant. That weird sensation she had felt so often when she was closing in on a criminal. She'd told him about it, but neither of them could explain it. Parker had always chalked it up to instincts. He wanted her to use them now.

Okay. She took a deep breath and tried to feel something.

She didn't.

"Not really."

Parker looked disappointed. But he was still determined. "I'd like to show you something. Are you up for a walk?"

"Sure."

"Are you certain? It's a bit of a jaunt. I don't want to push you if you're still weak."

She touched his handsome face and smiled. He always liked to baby her. "I'll let you know if I start to feel bad."

"Very well." He kissed her hand, got out of the car, and hurried around to the passenger side to open her door.

She had to laugh. "A gentleman, even in the middle of the woods."

"Good manners are appropriate everywhere."

"Guess so." And feeling a bounce in her step from a rush of love for him, she followed him onto the grass and under the trees.

The terrain in the forest was on the rugged side, to say the least. They worked their way through the pines and poplars, through thistles and creepers, over dead twigs and fallen logs. The ground descended in some spots, rose in others. They were near the Appalachians, alright.

Now Parker's camouflage getup made sense. And the jeans and boots he'd insisted she wear. She kind of liked the outdoorsy look on him.

As they walked along, he told her what he'd learned about Santana in Tampa and how it had led him to Gulf Shores. He told her about the Ukrainian he'd found there, and why he'd headed to Kentucky. She had a feeling he was leaving out a few pertinent details about the risks he'd taken to get that information. She would have said so, but who was she to talk about risk taking?

By the time they reached a clearing, she was a little winded.

Parker laid his hand against her back. "We need to stop and rest here. Are you feeling alright?"

She nodded. "I'm fine."

He led her to a log on the ground and eased her down. "Do you feel anything?"

"You mean am I lightheaded?"

His expression turned to concern. "Are you?"

Actually, she was feeling pretty good. The exercise must have washed away any remains of the drugs in her system. "No. I feel great."

He took a seat beside her. "That's a relief. But it's not what I meant. I want you to use those exquisite instincts of yours."

Of course, he did. The thing was, they didn't really work this way.

But she'd try.

After a moment of sitting, she stood up and took a few steps. She put her hands on her hips, and turned around in a circle to study the spot. It was just a campsite in a clearing. Somebody had built a fire in the middle of it a while ago. There was no one here now. No footprints. No trash. Just some burnt sticks of wood in a pile.

Her pulse was elevated, and her skin was still flushed from the hike, but that was about it.

She raised her palms. "Sorry, Parker."

Nodding, he got to his feet. "Can you go a little farther?"

She could go a lot farther, but she didn't want to worry him. "Yeah. I'm okay. Really."

"Very well. There's something else I want to show you."

They trudged through more forest, most of it going uphill now. After about half an hour, they reached the bank of a river.

Miranda sucked in a breath as she stared at the beautiful sight. The river was wide and looked pretty deep. Birds squawked in the trees, and along the other side of the bank, a thick green forest rose to a bright blue sky. Clear water rippled over rocks, and the air was fresh and invigorating.

"This is gorgeous, Parker."

"You're right, it is. But to be honest, until this moment, I hadn't noticed."

She turned to him. "What happened here?"

"I was searching the area with the FBI and the local police."

Her brows rose. "For Santana?"

"Let's sit down. You need to rest."

She let Parker settle her onto a thick patch of grass and listened to what he had to say. He told her they'd found a hunter on this spot with a dress shoe. He had built a fire at the campsite they'd just been to and found the shoe there.

"Wait. Did you say dress shoe?"

He nodded. "A Louis Vuitton."

That sounded like something that monster would wear. "Are you saying it belonged to Santana?"

"The bloodhounds seemed to think so. They responded to his scent."

She thought a moment and frowned. "What did the police use as a scent article?"

"I'll need to show you that."

They got up and walked back in the direction they'd come, going a little faster this time. The ground was mostly downhill, but the distance was too far for her taste.

At last they reached the Tesla.

Parker led her across the road to the other side and pointed down. "There."

Miranda followed his arm with her gaze and let out a gasp. "Holy mackerel. Is that the car that Ukrainian gave Santana?"

"It is. I almost missed it while I was driving this road yesterday, but I spotted the sheen off the rear bumper."

Parker was amazing.

The car was parked on a downward slope, its trunk sticking up in the air. It was old, out of style, and an ugly brown. A fitting vehicle for that bastard. "Did he run off the road?"

"It's out of gas. I concur with the authorities that Santana and Phineas pushed the vehicle off to the side so no one would find it."

"Until you did." She was truly proud of him. "And that was how the hounds got his scent."

"Correct."

Obviously he had been here a month ago, but Santana was nowhere around here now.

Now she fully understood what Parker was after. He wanted her to use her spidey sense to pinpoint where that monster was hiding in the area.

She was certainly up for that.

"Do you have a pair of gloves?"

"Always." He took them from his pocket and handed them to her.

She slipped them on and took a few downhill steps until she was at the cruiser's rear. She put her palms down on the trunk and took a deep breath. She closed her eyes and took another deep breath.

She thought of Santana's face. Imagining the feel of those nasty ants, she drew in a third breath.

No ants. No tingles. Nothing

She turned around and shrugged. "I don't feel anything, Parker."

The expression of hopelessness on his face broke her heart.

Then she looked around and took in her surroundings again. "Aren't there bears in these woods?"

Thoughtfully, he nodded. "Black bears, as well as coyotes."

"And snakes?"

"Copperheads and timber rattlers."

It was all making sense now. "You know Santana grew up in Boston, Parker. He was used to finery, being waited on, being taken care of."

"What are you saying?" But he knew.

She took off her gloves and handed them back to him. "Do you really think he had the skills to make it in these woods?"

Parker put the gloves back in his pocket. "That question had crossed my mind."

Of course, it had. But Parker had wanted a showdown, and now he wasn't going to get it. "Santana wasn't exactly a candidate for a survival show."

"And he was impaired."

"What do you mean?"

"The authorities have clear evidence he was limping."

From that fall on the island after his fight with Parker. That made her even more certain.

Parker rubbed his chin for a moment, then fixed her with a sharp eye. "You used the past tense."

"Right. I think he's gone."

"Gone." He said it as if he'd never quite believe it.

"It has to be so. It's the only logical conclusion." She stepped over to him and took both his hands in hers. "The only objective one."

He raised a brow at the word he'd so often used with her.

She had to smile at him. "Don't you see, Parker? Santana's gone. Really gone for good. He froze in these woods, or some snake or some bear found him and had a nice snack."

He thought it over for a moment, then his face turned grim. "Except for one thing."

"What?"

He let go of her hands. "Santana wasn't alone. Phineas was with him."

"Right." Looking back at the car, she pursed her lips at that one.

"And there's something else I haven't told you."

More secrets? She put her hands on her hips and narrowed an eye at him. "Spill."

Parker didn't smile. "Santana was armed."

"How do you know that?"

"We found an empty gun case for an antique Mauser parabellum IWA in his boat in Gulf Shores. Two magazines were missing as well."

"Is that a nine millimeter?"

He nodded. "It's a Luger."

"Okay." Scratching at her head, Miranda stared off into the trees and tried to imagine Santana limping around with a nerdy kid. Slowly, she began to nod her head. "Actually, that makes my scenario even more likely."

"Oh?"

"From what you've told me, Phineas was a nerdy geek with even fewer survival skills than Mr. Boston-Bred. They might have made it for a little while, but they wouldn't have lasted long."

Parker began to nod with her. "And when food and water grew scarce, Phineas became a liability."

"Right. And with that Luger, he'd be easy to get rid of."

Parker raised a brow. "And leave for the bears?"

'Uh huh." She peered through the trees again. "We can't say for sure how long he made it, but eventually Santana had to run out of bullets, and the tables turned. He couldn't outrun a bear with that limp. Especially with only one shoe."

Parker followed her gaze. "That does make sense. In this climate, whatever was left of the bodies would be decomposed by now."

Which was why the authorities hadn't found the bodies. She was sure of it. "They're gone. Both of them."

Parker was silent, pondering the idea.

She took his hands in hers again. "It makes perfect sense. And it means we don't have to be looking over our shoulders for the rest of our lives. We can really, really retire now. We're free, Parker. Free."

He drew in a breath and gave her a half smile.

It might take a while for him to get used to the idea, but right now she couldn't resist throwing her arms around his neck and giving him a big juicy kiss—right there in the middle of the forest.

"C'mon," she said after she'd broken away. "I'm hungry again. Don't they have good fried chicken in this state?"

"I believe they do."

She hurried up the hill and across the pavement to the car. "Make that chicken wings. With Diablo sauce."

He chuckled at that. "I'll see what we can find."

He got her settled in the passenger seat and came around to his side.

As he got in, she was glad to see the smile on his handsome face was still there.

There was also a gleam in his eye. "When we get back to Atlanta, would you like to go car shopping?"

She squealed out loud. "Car shopping? Are you finally going to let me replace your Lambo?"

"Up to now, I haven't felt the need. But just recently…"

"What?"

He ran his hands over the steering wheel. "I've had a hankering for a Tesla."

"We're getting a Tesla?" She let out a whoop. "I can't wait."

His smile sexier than ever, Parker gave her hand a squeeze, started the car, and sped off into the woods, giving her a thrill in the pit of her stomach.

The bad guys were done away with. Gone forever. Santana wasn't coming after them. At long last, they were safe. They were free. And now they were going home.

Together.

CHAPTER FIFTY-TWO

Carrying his duffle bag and a sack of fast food, he strolled under the trees along the Chicago neighborhood sidewalk, laughing to himself that nobody on the street had any idea who he was.

Or what he'd just done.

He turned into the walk that ran between two row houses and climbed the back stairs to the room he was renting on the second floor.

He opened the door with his key, stepped inside, and turned on the light.

It was warm in here. He'd left the heat on that morning before he went to the job he despised. And it smelled bad. He'd forgotten to take out the garbage.

But everything was just as he left it. No police. They didn't have a clue.

Still, things weren't perfect.

He stuffed his duffle bag in the bathroom. He'd clean his tools later. He'd already washed up at the kill site. He sat down at his kitchen table and began to eat his hamburger and fries.

Disgusted with himself, he reached for the notebook his mentor had left him and began to read again. He'd studied carefully. Tonight he'd practiced his new found techniques on his fifth victim. But he hadn't done it right.

Oh, he'd killed her. And he'd made her suffer for three long hours. But that wasn't long enough. His mentor could make them last for days.

And he didn't use the scaffolding his mentor required. He didn't use his tools either. He couldn't. He was too afraid to leave so much evidence.

And his independent nature made him rebel against rules and restrictions. But how else could he prepare himself for his ultimate task?

After all, he wasn't the man he'd once been. He barely recognized himself. He'd been transformed by the horrible ordeal he'd been through. And now he was someone else.

Sick of dwelling on his failures, he finished his food and threw the bag in the trash. Then he went over to the end of his bed and switched on the TV. The news was on. He always watched the news.

They were talking about his other four kills in the area. It was too soon for them to find tonight's body.

There was that chubby detective again and her boss, talking and saying nothing, and asking the public for help. They called him a slasher. How dare they say that about his work.

They were worthless.

He was about to turn the TV off, when a new headline flashed on the screen. "Neurosurgeon suspected of killing patients." Footage of a familiar face appeared as the reporter spoke. "We ran into Miranda Steele and her husband in a small Indiana town where they had tracked down a doctor they suspected of being a serial killer."

The camera switched to a local policeman. "It seems Ms. Steele had been in Oak Park, Illinois investigating the death of her mother when she got a clue that led her here to Doncaster. We're glad it did."

"More on this bizarre case after the break."

He shot up, turned off the TV, and slammed the remote down on the floor.

She had been here? Again? Not in the city this time, but a suburb? How dare she?

He grabbed a knife off his desk and stood before his collection of photos on the wall, his chest heaving.

He scanned the beautiful faces smiling down at him. They were all blondes. His mentor had been particular about that. Ash blondes, dirty blondes, platinum blondes.

And there in the middle of them was the raven-haired Miranda Steele with her cocky smirk. The photo he'd captured the last time he saw her on the news.

With a growl he raised the knife over his head and plunged it into her picture. He pulled it out and plunged it in again. He dug and dug and dug until he'd cut it to pieces. Just the way he was going to cut her.

Then he stepped back, shocked at what he had done.

It was too much. He tossed the knife back on the desk and pressed his hands to his head. He couldn't stand it. He had to do something. But what?

And then it came to him.

He would have to escalate his plans. He'd have to leave here.

But he'd have to be careful. Clean the place thoroughly. Scrub everything down. He couldn't leave any evidence behind. He was glad these rooms included a fireplace. He'd be busy tonight.

And as soon as he was ready, he'd go.

He would pack up his things and head for Atlanta tonight.

And then at last, he would put his plan into action.

THE END

ABOUT THE AUTHOR

Linsey Lanier writes chilling mystery-thrillers that keep you up at night.

Daughter of a WWII Navy Lieutenant, she has written fiction for more than fifteen years. She has authored over two dozen novels and short stories, including the popular Miranda's Rights Mystery series and the Miranda and Parker Mystery series. Someone Else's Daughter has received over 1,000 reviews and more than 500,000 downloads.

Linsey is a member of International Thriller Writers, Private Eye Writers of America, and Romance Writers of America, the Kiss of Death chapter. Her books have been nominated in several RWA-sponsored contests.

In her spare time, Linsey enjoys watching crime shows with her husband of over two decades and trying to figure out "who-dun-it." But her favorite activity is writing and creating entertaining new stories for her readers.

She's always working on a new book, currently books in the Miranda and Parker Mystery series (a continuation of the Miranda's Rights Mystery series). For alerts on her latest releases join Linsey's mailing list at linseylanier.com

For more of Linsey's books, visit her website at **www.linseylanier.com**

Proofreaad by

Donna Rich